Early Black Reformers

Early Black
Reformers

Other books in the History Firsthand series:

Early Black Reformers

James Tackach, *Book Editor*

Daniel Leone, *President*
Bonnie Szumski, *Publisher*
Scott Barbour, *Managing Editor*
David M. Haugen, *Series Editor*

GREENHAVEN
PRESS ®

THOMSON

™

GALE

San Diego • Detroit • New York • San Francisco • Cleveland
New Haven, Conn. • Waterville, Maine • London • Munich

LIBRARY OF CONGRESS CATALOGING-IN-PUBLICATION DATA

Early Black reformers / James Tackach, book editor.
    p. cm. — (History firsthand)
Includes bibliographical references and index.
ISBN 0-7377-1597-9 (alk. paper) — ISBN 0-7377-1598-7 (pbk. : alk. paper)
    1. African Americans—Civil rights—History—Sources. 2. African Americans—Politics and government—Sources. 3. African Americans—Social conditions—Sources. 4. Antislavery movements—United States—History—Sources. 5. African American civil rights workers—Biography. 6. African American political activists—Biography. 7. African American social reformers—Biography. 8. United States—Race relations—Sources. I. Tackach, James. II. Series.
E184.6 .E28 2003
323'.092'396073—dc21
                                        2002032972

Contents

Chapter 1: Black Abolitionists

Chapter 2: The Civil War and Reconstruction Eras

Chapter 3: Booker T. Washington and His Critics

Foreword

In his preface to a book on the events leading to the Civil War, Stephen B. Oates, the historian and biographer of Abraham Lincoln, John Brown, and other noteworthy American historical figures, explained the difficulty of writing history in the traditional third-person voice of the biographer and historian. "The trouble, I realized, was the detached third-person voice," wrote Oates. "It seemed to wring all the life out of my characters and the antebellum era." Indeed, how can a historian, even one as prominent as Oates, compete with the eloquent voices of Daniel Webster, Abraham Lincoln, Harriet Beecher Stowe, Frederick Douglass, and Robert E. Lee?

Oates's comment notwithstanding, every student of history, professional and amateur alike, can name a score of excellent accounts written in the traditional third-person voice of the historian that bring to life an event or an era and the people who lived through it. In *Battle Cry of Freedom*, James M. McPherson vividly re-creates the American Civil War. Barbara Tuchman's *The Guns of August* captures in sharp detail the tensions in Europe that led to the outbreak of World War I. Taylor Branch's *Parting the Waters* provides a detailed and dramatic account of the American Civil Rights Movement. The study of history would be impossible without such guiding texts.

Nonetheless, Oates's comment makes a compelling point. Often the most convincing tellers of history are those who lived through the event, the eyewitnesses who recorded their firsthand experiences in autobiographies, speeches, memoirs, journals, and letters. The Greenhaven Press History Firsthand series presents history through the words of first-person narrators. Each text in this series captures a significant historical era or event—the American Civil War, the

Great Depression, the Holocaust, the Roaring Twenties, the 1960s, the Vietnam War. Readers will investigate these historical eras and events by examining primary-source documents, authored by chroniclers both famous and little known. The texts in the History Firsthand series comprise the celebrated and familiar words of the presidents, generals, and famous men and women of letters who recorded their impressions for posterity, as well as the statements of the ordinary people who struggled to understand the storm of events around them—the foot soldiers who fought the great battles and their loved ones back home, the men and women who waited on the breadlines, the college students who marched in protest.

The texts in this series are particularly suited to students beginning serious historical study. By examining these firsthand documents, novice historians can begin to form their own insights and conclusions about the historical era or event under investigation. To aid the student in that process, the texts in the History Firsthand series include introductions that provide an overview of the era or event, timelines, and bibliographies that point the serious student toward key historical works for further study.

The study of history commences with an examination of words—the testimony of witnesses who lived through an era or event and left for future generations the task of making sense of their accounts. The Greenhaven Press History Firsthand series invites the beginner historian to commence the process of historical investigation by focusing on the words of those individuals who made history by living through it and recording their experiences firsthand.

Introduction: The Early Fight for Civil Rights

" "The words 'civil rights' summon up memories and images in modern minds of grainy television footage of packed mass meetings, firehoses and police dogs, of early 1960s peaceful protestors replaced over time by violent rioters, of soul-stirring oratory and bold actions, of assassination and death," writes Julian Bond, the 1960s African American civil rights activist. "But there were life and death struggles for civil rights long before the words were introduced into American homes on the evening news."[1] For many Americans, the civil rights movement refers to the effort during the 1950s and 1960s to end racial segregation and to extend to all Americans, regardless of race, the full rights of citizenship. But almost two centuries before Thurgood Marshall challenged school segregation laws in court, before Rosa Parks refused to surrender her seat on a Montgomery, Alabama, public bus, before the Reverend Martin Luther King Jr. delivered his eloquent and fiery speeches, black Americans were publicly agitating for their civil rights.

In a broader sense, the American civil rights movement refers to an effort begun even before Great Britain's American colonies had broken from their mother country and formed themselves into a democratic republic. The struggle commenced when the majority of African Americans were still enslaved—politically powerless victims of an institution deeply imbedded in the economy and culture of North America. An abolitionist movement with roots in the eighteenth century—a movement in which black Americans came to play an important role—gained momentum during the 1830s and, by the late 1850s, divided the nation, ultimately leading to a civil war that uprooted slavery from

American soil. The crusade that ended slavery developed into a post–Civil War campaign to secure citizenship rights for the newly freed slaves. That movement continued into the twentieth century and blossomed into the civil rights movement that King came to lead during the mid-1950s. The leaders of this broad, two-centuries-long civil rights movement came from all walks of life and all social classes: slaves and freemen; the illiterate and highly literate; the formally educated and the self-taught; laborers; lawyers; clergymen; and entrepreneurs. Both men and women rose to positions of leadership within the movement. Although these reformers advanced toward a single goal—the full rights of citizenship for all African Americans—they marched not in lockstep. They articulated common messages—the abolition of slavery, the right to vote, social and political equality, educational and economic opportunity—but their means and tactics varied, often causing clashes among and developing deep rifts within the civil rights leadership. Their varied firsthand experiences reveal a broad spectrum of viewpoints and a compelling story of perseverance and persistence in the most trying of circumstances. These early black reformers marched unsteadily against stiff opposition toward a new dawn.

The Abolitionist Crusade

Slavery took root in North America in 1619, when Dutch traders landed at the British settlement in Jamestown, Virginia, with a score of Africans kidnapped from their homeland—slaves to be sold as field hands to Jamestown landowners. Between 1619 and 1808, when the U.S. Congress outlawed the importation of slaves, several hundred thousand Africans were brought to America and enslaved for life. Their descendants became slaves at birth, ensuring the perpetuation of the institution of slavery. The census of 1800 listed 893,602 slaves in the United States. By 1860 that number had increased to almost 4 million.

Opposition to slavery developed during the seventeenth century, but the oldest surviving abolitionist document has a publication date of 1700: *The Selling of Joseph,* an antislavery pamphlet written by Samuel Sewall, a Puritan magistrate of Massachusetts. Other abolitionist advocates emerged during the eighteenth century—the Puritan minister Cotton Mather, the Quaker minister John Woolman, Benjamin Franklin, John Adams, the former slave Olaudah Equiano—but an organized national abolitionist movement did not begin until the 1830s, when William Lloyd Garrison, a white Massachusetts newspaper editor, commenced publication of *The Liberator* and established the American Anti-Slavery Society.

Garrison welcomed blacks into his campaign. The abolitionist movement was the first American reform movement in which African Americans played a key role. Garrison recruited articulate former slaves like Frederick Douglass to speak at antislavery rallies and contribute their writings to *The Liberator*. In Garrison's abolitionist crusade, former slaves served as eyewitnesses who could comment firsthand on slavery's atrocities. Former slaves could awaken complacent Americans to the evils of the institution that was already dividing the nation and threatening civil unrest.

Black Abolitionist Leaders

The Civil War historian James M. McPherson states that "there were almost as many kinds of abolitionists as there were individuals in the movement."[2] McPherson identifies three distinct factions within the abolitionist movement: the non-church-oriented Garrisonians; the evangelicals, who worked through their churches, offering a religious critique of slavery; and the political abolitionists, who strived to achieve their goal by working within the existing political structure. Add to these factions the radical abolitionists, whose goal was to eradicate slavery by means of violent revolution. Black abolitionists could be found within each faction.

Olaudah Equiano directed his attack against the international slave trade to the queen of England, imploring her to support antislavery bills being discussed in Parliament:

I presume . . . gracious Queen, to implore your interposition with

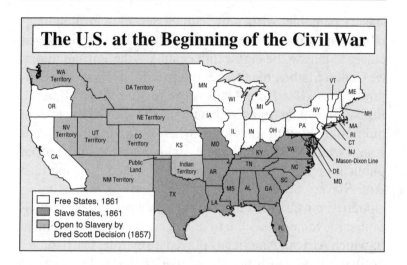

The U.S. at the Beginning of the Civil War

WA Territory
OR
NV Territory
UT Territory
CA
DA Territory
NE Territory
CO Territory
Public Land
NM Territory
MN
WI
IA
KS
MO
Indian Territory
AR
TX
LA
MI
IL
IN
OH
KY
TN
MS
AL
GA
VA
NC
SC
FL
PA
NY
VT
ME
NH
MA
RI
CT
NJ
DE
MD
Mason-Dixon Line

☐ Free States, 1861
■ Slave States, 1861
☐ Open to Slavery by Dred Scott Decision (1857)

your royal consort, in favor of the wretched Africans; that, by your Majesty's benevolent influence, a period may now be put to their misery; and that they may be raised from the condition of brutes, to which they are at present degraded, to the rights and situation of freemen, and admitted to partake of the blessings of your Majesty's happy government.[3]

Frederick Douglass joined the Garrisonians (though he and Garrison would later split and work in parallel but separate spheres). David Walker leveled a religious attack against slavery, warning of a stern and just God who "will surely destroy" the slaveholders "to show his disapprobation."[4] Frances Watkins Harper used poetry as the medium for her call for abolition.

But not all black abolitionists believed that slavery could be uprooted through moral suasion or through channels within the existing political system. Many black abolitionists challenged the laws protecting slavery by illegally participating in the Underground Railroad. Other black abolitionists completely rejected political and religious approaches to abolition, opting instead for armed revolt. A slave riot occurred in New York City in 1712, resulting in the deaths of nine whites. A slave revolt involving about eighty armed slaves erupted on a South Carolina plantation in 1739. A battle with armed whites resulted in the deaths of forty-four slaves and twenty-one whites. In 1800 Gabriel and Martin Prosser, slave brothers living in Virginia, planned an attack on a Richmond arsenal that failed. In 1821 a religious Charlestown, South Carolina, slave named Denmark Vesey planned a holy war against slavery, but his plot was detected, and Vesey was executed.

By far the best-known slave revolt was directed by Nat Turner in Southampton County, Virginia, in August 1831. Turner, a self-ordained slave minister, claimed that he had received a command from the Almighty to smite the slave-holder and free the slave:

> And on the 12th of May, 1828, I heard a loud noise in the heavens, and the Spirit instantly appeared to me and said the Serpent was loosened, and Christ had laid down the yoke he had borne for the sins of men, and that I should take it on and fight against the Serpent, for the time was fast approaching when the first should be last and the last should be first.[5]

Turner commenced his revolt in August 1831. In a single night of terror, Turner and his followers killed about sixty slave owners and their family members. The revolt was quickly suppressed, and Turner was captured, tried, and executed. But his effort inspired another militant abolitionist, John Brown, a white Ohioan, whose assault on the federal arsenal at Harpers Ferry, Virginia, in 1859—for the purpose of arming slaves and igniting a slave rebellion—is often cited as the event that put the nation on the track toward civil war.

The War Against Slavery

In President Abraham Lincoln's mind, the Civil War began as a war to force the rebellious Southern states back into the Union from which they tried to separate themselves. On January 1, 1863, after almost two years of war, however, Lincoln signed the Emancipation Proclamation, freeing the slaves in the states in rebellion against the Union, and the war became a conflict to end American slavery. If the South won its independence, slavery would remain in place in the rebellious states; if the North won, the rebellious states would be forced back into the Union without slavery.

Abolitionists like Senator Charles Sumner of Massachusetts, Congressman Thaddeus Stevens of Pennsylvania, and Frederick Douglass played a key role in prompting Lincoln to issue the Emancipation Proclamation. During the early part of the war, Douglass's fiery abolitionist editorials in *Douglass' Monthly* urged the reluctant president to make emancipation a goal of the war. Douglass also pressed Lincoln to allow black men to enlist in the Union army. Lincoln's Emancipation Proclamation turned Douglass's demands into federal policy. The emancipation decree freed the slaves in states in rebellion and invited free black men to join the Union army and navy. During the next two years, almost two hundred thousand African Americans answered Lincoln's call—a fresh supply of manpower that helped turn the tide of the Civil War in the North's favor.

The North's victory in the war spelled the abolition of American slavery. The Thirteenth Amendment to the U.S. Constitution, enacted in December 1865, asserts that "neither slavery nor involuntary servitude . . . shall exist within the United States, or any place subject to their jurisdiction." The passage of this amendment was a stunning victory for Douglass, Harper, and other African American abolitionists, some of whom had spent most of their own lives in bondage.

A Post–Civil War Civil Rights Movement

Historians have debated the extent to which the abolitionists advanced the post–Civil War struggle for citizenship rights for the freed slaves. Some Reconstruction historians argue that abolitionists abandoned the effort for civil rights for African Americans after the passage of the Thirteenth Amendment. McPherson disagrees, asserting that "abolitionists led the campaign for equal rights after emancipation and launched the movement for education of the freedmen."[6] Certainly that is the case with the black abolitionists, who saw the end of slavery as only a single step in a movement whose goal was to make African Americans full participants in the American democracy. Douglass, the great African

American abolitionist leader, emerged as the principal spokesman for full citizenship rights for African Americans during the post–Civil War era.

But Douglass's ideas clashed with those of other Reconstruction-era black civil rights activists, especially with feminists who saw in the turbulence of Reconstruction an opportunity to push for women's suffrage. Frances Watkins Harper and Ida B. Wells-Barnett joined with white women's suffrage advocates like Elizabeth Cady Stanton and Susan B. Anthony to advance their cause. Douglass, who always spoke in favor of a woman's right to vote, split with the suffrage women because he feared that their movement would obscure his effort to secure the voting rights for the newly freed black men, who, Douglass believed, needed the vote more than women did. "I am now devoting myself to a cause not more sacred, certainly urgent [than women's suffrage], because it is life and death to the long-enslaved people of this country; and this is: Negro suffrage," Douglass wrote to a friend involved in the women's suffrage movement in 1868. "While the Negro is mobbed, beaten, shot, stabbed, hanged, burnt, and is the target of all that is malignant in the North and all that is murderous in the South his claims may be preferred by me without exposing in any wise myself to the imputation of narrowness or meanness towards the cause of women."[7]

Douglass, an integrationist, also sparred with post–Civil War black leaders who advocated the establishment of a separate state within the United States for black citizens, an idea once advanced by Sojourner Truth, the abolitionist orator, during Reconstruction. Some African American reformers believed that black citizens could achieve full citizenship rights only in a separate state or nation of their own. Douglass believed that the future of African Americans rested in a thoroughly integrated nation in which blacks and whites would have equal political and social rights as well as equal educational and economic opportunities.

The civil rights movement that took place during Reconstruction resulted in some tangible gains for black Americans. In 1868 the Fourteenth Amendment to the U.S. Constitution was adopted, making blacks citizens of the United States and of their states of residence and guaranteeing them "equal protection of the laws." Two years later, the Fifteenth Amendment was approved, its key clause stating that "the right of citizens of the United States to vote shall not be denied or abridged by the United States or by any State on account of race, color, or previous condition of servitude." Congress also tried to extend citizenship rights to the newly freed slaves by passing the Civil Rights Acts of 1866 and 1875.

Despite the passage of this impressive legislation, the United States, at the end of the nineteenth century, remained a racially divided nation. In 1896 the United States Supreme Court, in the landmark case of *Plessy v. Ferguson,* established the "separate-but-equal" principle; laws that separated the races in social settings were deemed constitutional as long as the conditions and facilities for each race were equal. This court ruling led to the passage of the so-called Jim Crow laws that rigidly segregated the races, establishing separate public schools, separate seating in train cars, and separate beaches and parks. The Jim Crow era lasted until the 1960s.

The Emergence of Booker T. Washington and W.E.B. DuBois

After the death of Frederick Douglass in 1895, Booker T. Washington, a former slave who had become the president of the Tuskegee Institute in Alabama, and William Edward Burghardt DuBois, a Harvard-educated Massachusetts native born after the Civil War, emerged as leaders in the effort to secure citizenship rights for African Americans. Their goals might have been similar, but their solutions for America's troubling racial problems at the turn of the twentieth century differed greatly.

Washington, who had risen to his position at Tuskegee through hard work, perseverance, and deference to white superiors, advocated a policy of gradualism. According to Washington, African Americans should not concern themselves with immediate political and social equality but instead should concentrate their efforts on achieving economic independence by mastering vital trades such as farming, masonry, carpentry, mechanics, and nursing. By acquiring the skills needed to become successful farmers and tradesmen, black Americans would come to occupy an important place in the U.S. economy. Social and political rights like voting would gradually follow. To achieve his goals, Washington envisioned a national network of schools like the Tuskegee Institute to train young black people and prepare them to achieve economic self-reliance. In his famous Atlanta Exposition address, delivered on September 18, 1895, Washington advised his fellow African Americans, "It is at the bottom of life we must begin, and not at the top." Regarding the struggle for racial equality, he stated, "The wisest among my race understand that the agitation of questions of social equality is the extremest folly, and that progress in the enjoyment of all the privileges that will come to us must be the result of severe and constant struggle rather than of artificial forcing."[8]

In 1895, the year of Washington's Atlanta address and Douglass's death, W.E.B. DuBois received his Ph.D. from Harvard University and began a remarkable public career that lasted until his death in the 1960s. He had attended integrated schools and had grown to adulthood in Massachusetts, arguably the most progressive state in the Union in terms of racial attitudes. In his first major scholarly publication, *The Souls of Black Folk,* published in 1903, DuBois attacked Washington's philosophy of gradualism: "Mr. Washington represents in Negro thought the old attitude of adjustment and submission; . . . Mr. Washington's programme practically accepts the alleged inferiority of the Negro races."[9] DuBois accused Washington of asking black people to sacrifice political power, civil rights, and opportunities for higher education. Instead, DuBois demanded for African Americans the right to vote, civic equality, and the education of youth according to their ability.

Early twentieth-century African American civil rights

leaders fell in line with Washington or DuBois. Both men went on to have influential careers. Washington met with presidents, politicians, and business leaders across the United States to carry his message and advance his philosophy. DuBois formed the National Association for the Advancement of Colored People (NAACP), the organization that would ultimately launch a lethal attack on Jim Crow.

Early Twentieth-Century Black Reformers

Washington died in 1915. DuBois continued to be an important voice of reform in the African American community for many years. He was joined, and sometimes opposed, by other dynamic African American civil rights leaders who tackled a variety of race-related issues and shaped reform policies during the first three decades of the twentieth century. Ida B. Wells-Barnett, a former slave who played a role in the formation of the NAACP, campaigned tirelessly for laws to prevent lynching—a practice that led to the deaths of thousands of innocent blacks in the South (and many in the North as well)—during the late nineteenth and early twentieth centuries.

Marcus Garvey offered a challenge to the NAACP's drive to break down the barriers of segregation and fully integrate American society. Garvey, a native of Jamaica, born in 1887, advocated the establishment of a separate and economically independent black society, either within the United States or in Africa. He urged European nations to cease their control of or interference with Africa's affairs. To advance his cause, Garvey, during the early 1920s, founded the Universal Negro Improvement Association, through which he launched several business ventures, including Black Star Line, an international shipping company, and New Factories Corporation, an organization designed to promote black-owned businesses. Garvey realized that black people constituted a sizable bloc of purchasing power. He urged black consumers to purchase products manufactured by black workers and sold by black marketers—a practice that would create wealth in the black community.

During the 1930s some black civil rights reformers responded to the appeals of the American Socialist and Communist Parties. In 1929 the United States entered the Great Depression, an economic turndown that threatened to break the nation's capitalist economic system. Capitalism had failed, and many Americans looked to the Socialists and Communists for solutions to the country's economic problems. The depression caused particularly great pain in black communities. Black workers were usually the first to lose their jobs when layoffs were announced. A severe drought in much of the rural South left many black sharecroppers facing famine. The Socialists and Communists reached out to black Americans, asserting that the nation's two established political parties—the Democrats and Republicans—had completely neglected the interests of African Americans. The African American author Richard Wright joined the Communist Party in 1933 and published articles in *New Masses* and other Socialist-leaning periodicals.

World War II Provides a Challenge to Jim Crow

The Great Depression lasted until the start of World War II. When the nation geared up for war with Germany and Japan, American workers went back to the factories and worked overtime to create the machinery of war. The nation united to fight common enemies, and African American leaders like DuBois urged black Americans to support the nation's war effort. In September 1940, more than a year before the United States entered World War II, the NAACP announced that black Americans would back their nation if it entered the European conflict: "Though thirteen million Negroes have more often than not been denied democracy, they are American citizens and will as in every war give unqualified support to the protection of their country."[10]

Thousands of African American soldiers, sailors, airmen, and nurses took part in World War II. They fought in a war to defeat the racist regime of Adolf Hitler in Nazi Germany. These African American war veterans returned home, however, to an American society still rigidly divided along racial lines. Reflecting on the war's effect on the African American's place in American society, Constance Baker Motley, an NAACP attorney, stated,

> I think people became more aware that something had to be done about the fact that black servicemen were overseas dying for this country, and . . . they would be coming home to a situation that said, in effect, You're a second-class citizen. You can't go to school with white children, or your children can't. You can't stay in a hotel or eat in a restaurant because you're black.[11]

Black reformers were quick to grasp the opportunities offered by the war. Just as the war ended, Jackie Robinson, an army veteran and an outstanding shortstop on the Kansas City Monarchs of the Negro League, signed a minor league contract with the Brooklyn Dodgers. In April 1947, after two terrific minor league seasons, Robinson took the field for the Dodgers. Major league baseball, a bastion of white supremacy, was integrated. Robinson's courage, perseverance, and success opened the major league door for other black baseball players and provided the nation with an example of how racial integration could peacefully take place. A year after Robinson successfully integrated major league baseball, President Harry S. Truman integrated the U.S. armed forces.

Challenging Jim Crow Schools

Even before the war, the NAACP's Legal Defense Fund had begun challenging school segregation laws. The fund's leading attorney, Thurgood Marshall, first attacked state laws that denied black students admission to graduate programs in state colleges and universities. Marshall had been denied admission to the University of Maryland School of Law because the school did not admit black students. In 1937, in the case of *Murray v. Maryland,* Marshall forced the University of Maryland to admit qualified black law students. In 1938 Marshall forced the University of Missouri School of Law to do the same. In 1950 the Supreme Court invalidated a Texas law that prevented black students from enrolling at the University of Texas School of Law in a case brought forward by Marshall.

In the aftermath of World War II, the NAACP decided to challenge the laws that segregated public elementary and high schools. The organization backed groups of black students and parents in Virginia, Delaware, Kansas, and South Carolina who wished to challenge state laws that relegated black students to substandard all-black schools. NAACP attorneys filed lawsuits in these four states, and in Washington, D.C., as well, arguing that the segregated schools denied black students the equal protection of the laws guaranteed by the Fourteenth Amendment. The schools established for black students had inferior facilities—some even lacked indoor plumbing—and lacked laboratory equipment and sufficient library holdings. Many teachers in black schools lacked proper training and educational credentials.

In 1954 the Supreme Court ruled on these cases in the decision titled *Brown v. Board of Education of Topeka, Kansas:* "We conclude that in the field of public education the doctrine of 'separate but equal' has no place. Separate educational facilities are inherently unequal." The Court ordered a gradual school desegregation program that would ultimately put an end to Jim Crow education.

A Legal Precedent

The Supreme Court's decision in the *Brown* case not only began the phasing out of segregated public education but also provided civil rights reformers with a legal precedent with which to challenge other segregation laws. In 1955 a U.S. district court ruled that the city of Baltimore could no longer segregate its public beaches, parks, or recreational facilities. Later that year, the Supreme Court struck down an Atlanta city ordinance that prevented blacks from using the city's public golf course. Jim Crow soon was on the run throughout the nation.

King called the *Brown* decision "an exit sign that suddenly appeared to one who had walked through a long and desolate corridor," a "decision [that] came as a way out of the darkness of segregation."[12] Rosa Parks invoked the spirit of *Brown* when she refused to surrender her seat on a Montgomery, Alabama, public bus in December 1955: Public facilities must be available for use by all citizens on an equal basis. King came to lead the Montgomery bus boycott, which became his first major civil rights victory when the Supreme Court invalidated Montgomery's bus-seating laws.

The Civil Rights Movement

King's victory in Montgomery prompted him to launch an attack on Jim Crow that eventually encompassed the entire South. He became the recognized leader of the civil rights movement that rid the United States of racial segregation sanctioned by law. His movement also enabled black citizens in the South to exercise their right to register and vote. The civil rights movement changed the political and social face of the nation.

Even during King's civil rights movement, however, black leaders often clashed over both goals and tactics. Malcolm X and his Black Muslims challenged King's integrationist message, calling for a separate black nation and economic system. The Black Panther Party, established during the mid-1960s, rejected King's call for nonviolent protest; Black Panthers armed themselves and fought several bloody battles with law enforcement officials. These civil rights activists of the King era followed the tradition of the early black reformers—abolitionists and civil rights advocates whose conflicting voices laid the groundwork for almost two centuries of civil rights reforms.

Notes

1. Julian Bond, introduction to *The Civil Rights Movement: An Eyewitness History* by Sanford Wexler. New York: Facts On File, 1993, p. ix.
2. James M. McPherson, *The Abolitionist Legacy: From Reconstruction to the NAACP.* Princeton, NJ: Princeton University Press, 1975, pp. 4–5.

3. Olaudah Equiano, *The Interesting Narrative of the Life of Olaudah Equiano*, ed. Werner Sollors. New York: W.W. Norton, 2001, p. 175.

4. David Walker, *David Walker's Appeal, in Four Articles*. New York: Hill and Wang, 1965, p. 69.

5. Kenneth S. Greenberg, *The Confessions of Nat Turner and Related Documents*. Boston: Bedford Books of St. Martin's, 1996, pp. 47–48.

6. McPherson, *The Abolitionist Legacy*, p. 3.

7. Frederick Douglass, *Selected Speeches and Writings*, ed. Philip S. Foner. Chicago: Lawrence Hill Books, 1999, p. 600.

8. Booker T. Washington, *Up from Slavery and Other Early Black Narratives*. New York: Doubleday, 1998, pp. 161, 163.

9. W.E.B. DuBois, *The Souls of Black Folk*. New York: Penguin Books, 1989, p. 43.

10. Quoted in Wexler, *The Civil Rights Movement*, p. 26.

11. Quoted in Henry Hampton and Steve Fayer, *Voices of Freedom: An Oral History of the Civil Rights Movement from the 1950s Through the 1980s*. New York: Bantam Books, 1990, p. xxv.

12. Martin Luther King Jr., *I Have a Dream: Writings and Speeches That Changed the World*, ed. James M. Washington. San Francisco: HarperSanFrancisco, 1992, p. 65.

Chapter 1

Black Abolitionists

Chapter Preface

The abolitionist movement was the first American reform movement in which black people played a major role. Former slaves such as Olaudah Equiano and Frederick Douglass and African American freemen such as David Walker and Frances Watkins Harper were important voices in the abolitionist crusade. The first American abolitionists, however, were whites. Before the American Revolution, most African Americans were slaves, and the few freemen lacked the tools necessary to initiate or direct any reform movement. Most could neither read nor write, and they played no role in the political life of colonial America or in the new American republic.

The first black abolitionists whose voices were heard emerged during the late eighteenth century. These were solitary protesters unconnected to any national antislavery movement. By the 1830s, however, an organized national abolitionist movement had formed in the United States, and African Americans began joining it in large numbers. That movement was spearheaded by whites—William Lloyd Garrison, Theodore Weld, William Ellery Channing, Lyman Beecher—but African Americans such as Douglass and Harper would come to play an important and effective role in that movement. They joined antislavery societies, produced antislavery literary texts, wrote for and published abolitionist newspapers, and demonstrated their oratory skills at antislavery rallies and conventions.

All African American abolitionists did not read from the same script. Some advocated peaceful political solutions to the problem of slavery; others promoted an armed revolt against slaveholders. Many used religion to bolster their argument for the abolition of American slavery. Black abolitionists who were former slaves often related their firsthand experiences in bondage in their speeches and writings, something that white abolitionists could not do. Some African American abolitionists also wrote and spoke of prejudices within the abolitionist movement as they found themselves to be second-class residents within a movement that fought for their right to live as free citizens.

After the start of the Civil War in 1861, the abolitionists continued to promote their cause by attempting to convince President Abraham Lincoln that the fractured Union could not be effectively reunited with slavery in place. On January 1, 1863, Lincoln issued the Emancipation Proclamation, which freed the slaves in the states that had seceded from the Union. By the war's end, Congress had approved the Thirteenth Amendment to the U.S. Constitution, which outlawed slavery throughout the United States and its territories.

A Condemnation of the International Slave Trade

Olaudah Equiano

> Olaudah Equiano was born on the west coast of Africa in
> around 1745. When he was eleven years old, he was kid-
> napped by slave traders, taken aboard a slave ship bound for
> America, and sold into slavery. He was freed in 1766 and
> eventually settled in Great Britain, where he attained literacy
> and became active in the British antislavery movement. In
> 1789, Equiano published his autobiography, *The Interesting
> Narrative of the Life of Olaudah Equiano, or Gustavus Vassa,
> the African,* the first American slave narrative written by a
> former slave. The focus of Equiano's antislavery activism was
> the international slave trade. For the last two decades of his
> life, Equiano lobbied the British government to outlaw inter-
> continental slave trading. This excerpt from Equiano's auto-
> biography shows that Equiano's critique of the slave trade
> was based on his own nightmarish experience as a child.

I have already acquainted the reader with the time and
place of my birth. My father, besides many slaves, had a
numerous family, of which seven lived to grow up, including myself and a sister, who was the only daughter. As I was
the youngest of the sons, I became, of course, the greatest
favourite with my mother, and was always with her; and she
used to take particular pains to form my mind. I was trained

Olaudah Equiano, *The Interesting Narrative of the Life of Olaudah Equiano, or Gustavus
Vassa, the African, Written by Himself,* edited by Werner Sollors, New York: W.W. Norton, 2001.

up from my earliest years in the art of war; my daily exercise was shooting and throwing javelins; and my mother adorned me with emblems, after the manner of our greatest warriors. In this way I grew up till I was turned the age of eleven, when an end was put to my happiness in the following manner:—Generally when the grown people in the neighborhood were gone far in the fields to labour, the children assembled together in some of the neighbours' premises to play; and commonly some of us used to get up a tree to look out for any assailant, or kidnapper, that might come upon us; for they sometimes took those opportunities of our parents' absence to attack and carry off as many as they could seize. One day, as I was watching at the top of a tree in our yard, I saw one of those people come into the yard of our next neighbour but one, to kidnap, there being many stout young people in it. Immediately on this I gave the alarm of the rogue, and he was surrounded by the stoutest of them, who entangled him with cords, so that he could not escape till some of the grown people came and secured him. But alas! ere long it was my fate to be thus attacked, and to be carried off, when none of the grown people were nigh.

Kidnapped

One day, when all our people were gone out to their works as usual, and only I and my dear sister were left to mind the house, two men and a woman got over our walls, and in a moment seized us both, and, without giving us time to cry out, or make resistance, they stopped our mouths, and ran off with us into the nearest wood. Here they tied our hands, and continued to carry us as far as they could, till night came on, when we reached a small house, where the robbers halted for refreshment, and spent the night. We were then unbound, but were unable to take any food; and, being quite overpowered by fatigue and grief, our only relief was some sleep, which allayed our misfortune for a short time. The next morning we left the house, and continued travelling all the day. For a long time we had kept the woods, but at last we came into a road which I believed I knew. I had now some hopes of being delivered; for we had advanced but a little way before I discovered some people at a distance, on which I began to cry out for their assistance: but my cries had no other effect than to make them tie me faster and stop my mouth, and then they put me into a large sack. They also stopped my sister's mouth, and tied her hands; and in this manner we proceeded till we were out of the sight of these people. When we went to rest the following night they offered us some victuals; but we refused it; and the only comfort we had was in being in one another's arms all that night, and bathing each other with our tears. But alas! we were soon deprived of even the small comfort of weeping together. The next day proved a day of greater sorrow than I had yet experienced; for my sister and I were then separated, while we lay clasped in each other's arms. It was in vain that we besought them not to part us; she was torn from me, and immediately carried away, while I was left in a state of distraction not to be described. . . .

I continued to travel, sometimes by land, sometimes by water, through different countries and various nations, till, at the end of six or seven months after I had been kidnapped, I arrived at the sea coast. It would be tedious and uninteresting to relate all the incidents which befell me during this journey, and which I have not yet forgotten; of the various hands I passed through, and the manners and customs of all the different people among whom I lived: I shall therefore only observe, that in all the places where I was the soil was exceedingly rich; the pomkins, eadas, plantains, yams, &c. &c. were in great abundance, and of incredible size. There were also vast quantities of different gums, though not used for any purpose; and every where a great deal of tobacco. The cotton even grew quite wild; and there was plenty of red-wood. I saw no mechanics [craftsmen] whatever in all the way, except such as I have mentioned. The chief employment in all these countries was agriculture, and both the males and females, as with us, were brought up to it, and trained in the arts of war.

The Slave Ship

The first object which saluted my eyes when I arrived on the coast was the sea, and a slave ship, which was then riding at anchor, and waiting for its cargo. These filled me with astonishment, which was soon converted into terror when I was carried on board. I was immediately handled and tossed up to see if I were sound by some of the crew; and I was now persuaded that I had gotten into a world of bad spirits, and that they were going to kill me. Their complexions too differing so much from ours, their long hair, and the language they spoke, (which was very different from any I had ever heard) united to confirm me in this belief. Indeed such were the horrors of my views and fears at the moment, that, if ten thousand worlds had been my own, I would have freely parted with them all to have exchanged my condition with that of the meanest slave in my own country. When I looked round the ship too and saw a large furnace or copper boiling, and a multitude of black people of every description chained together, every one of their countenances expressing dejection and sorrow, I no longer doubted of my fate; and, quite overpowered with horror and anguish, I fell motionless on the deck and fainted. When I recovered a little I found some black people about me, who I believed were some of those who brought me on board, and had been receiving their pay; they talked to me in order to cheer me, but all in vain. I asked them if we were not to be eaten by those white men with horrible looks, red faces, and loose hair. They told me I was not; and one of the crew brought me a small portion of spirituous liquor in a wine glass; but, being afraid of him, I would not take it out of his hand. One of the blacks therefore took it from him and gave it to me, and I took a little down my palate, which, instead of reviving me, as they thought it would, threw me into the greatest consternation at the strange feeling it produced, having never tasted any such liquor before. Soon after this the blacks who brought me on board went off, and left me abandoned to despair. I now saw myself deprived of all chance of returning to my native country, or even the least glimpse of hope of gaining the shore, which I now considered as friendly; and I even wished for my former slavery in preference to my present situation, which was filled with horrors of every kind, still heightened by my ignorance of what I was to undergo. I was not long suffered to indulge my grief; I was soon put down under the decks, and there I received such a salutation in my nostrils as I had never experienced in my life: so that, with the loathsomeness of the stench, and crying together, I became so sick and low that I was not able to eat, nor had I the

Olaudah Equiano

least desire to taste any thing. I now wished for the last friend, death, to relieve me; but soon, to my grief, two of the white men offered me eatables; and, on my refusing to eat, one of them held me fast by the hands, and laid me across I think the windlass, and tied my feet, while the other flogged me severely. I had never experienced any thing of this kind before; and although, not being used to the water, I naturally feared that element the first time I saw it, yet nevertheless, could I have got over the nettings, I would have jumped over the side, but I could not; and, besides, the crew used to watch us very closely who were not chained down to the decks, lest we should leap into the water: and I have seen some of these poor African prisoners most severely cut for attempting to do so, and hourly whipped for not eating. This indeed was often the case with myself. In a little time after, amongst the poor chained men, I found some of my own nation, which in a small degree gave ease to my mind. I inquired of these what was to be done with us; they gave me to understand we were to be carried to these white people's country to work for them. I then was a little revived, and thought, if it were no worse than working, my situation was not so desperate: but still I feared I should be put to death, the white people looked and acted, as I thought, in so savage a manner; for I had never seen among any people such instances of brutal cruelty; and this not only shewn towards us blacks, but also to some of the whites themselves. One white man in particular I saw, when we were permitted to be on deck, flogged so unmercifully with a large rope near the foremast, that he died in consequence of it; and they tossed him over the side as they would have done a brute. This made me fear these people the more; and I expected nothing less than to be treated in the same manner. I could not help expressing my fears and apprehensions to some of my countrymen: I asked them if these people had no country, but lived in this hollow place (the ship): they told me they did not, but came from a distant one. "Then," said I, "how comes it in all our country we never heard of them?" They told me because they lived so very far off. I then asked where were their women? had they any like themselves? I was told they had: "and why," said I, "do we not see them?" they answered, because they were left behind. I asked how the vessel could go? they told me they could not tell; but that there were cloths put upon the masts by the help of the ropes I saw, and then the vessel went on; and the white men had some spell or magic they put in the water when they liked in order to stop the vessel. I was exceedingly amazed at this account, and really thought they were spirits. I therefore wished much to be from amongst them, for I expected they would sacrifice me: but my wishes were vain; for we were so quartered that it was impossible for any of us to make our escape. While we stayed on the coast I was mostly on deck; and one day, to my great astonishment, I saw one of these vessels coming in with the sails up. As soon as the whites saw it, they gave a great shout, at which we were amazed; and the more so as the vessel appeared larger by approaching nearer. At last she came to an anchor in my sight, and when the anchor was let go I and my countrymen who saw it were lost in astonishment to observe the vessel stop; and were now convinced it was done by magic. Soon after this the other ship got her boats out, and they came on board of us, and the people of both ships seemed very glad to see each other. Several of the strangers also shook hands with us black people, and made motions with their hands, signifying I suppose we were to go to their country; but we did not understand them. At last, when the ship we were in had got in all her cargo, they made ready with many fearful noises, and we were all put under deck, so that we could not see how they managed the vessel. But this disappointment was the least of my sorrow.

Deplorable Conditions

The stench of the hold while we were on the coast was so intolerably loathsome, that it was dangerous to remain there for any time, and some of us had been permitted to stay on the deck for the fresh air; but now that the whole ship's cargo were confined together, it became absolutely pestilential. The closeness of the place, and the heat of the climate, added to the number in the ship, which was so crowded that each had scarcely room to turn himself, almost suffocated us. This produced copious perspirations, so that the air soon became unfit for respiration, from a variety of loathsome smells, and brought on a sickness among the slaves, of which many died, thus falling victims to the improvident avarice, as I may call it, of their purchasers. This wretched situation was again aggravated by the galling of the chains, now become insupportable; and the filth of the necessary tubs [toilets], into which the children often fell, and were almost suffocated. The shrieks of the women, and the groans of the dying, rendered the whole a scene of horror almost inconceivable. Happily perhaps for myself I was soon reduced so low here that it was thought necessary to keep me almost always on deck; and from my extreme youth I was not put in fetters. In this situation I expected every hour to share the fate of my companions, some of whom were almost daily brought upon deck at the point of death, which I began to hope would soon put an end to my miseries. Often did I think many of the inhabitants of the deep much more happy than myself. I envied them the freedom they enjoyed, and as often wished I could change my condition for theirs. Every circumstance I met with served only to render my state more painful, and heighten my apprehensions, and my opinion of the cruelty of the whites. One day they had taken a number of fishes; and when they had killed and satisfied themselves with as many as they thought fit, to our astonishment who were on the deck, rather than give any of them to us to eat as we expected, they tossed the remaining fish into the sea again, although we begged and prayed for some as well as we could, but in vain; and some of my countrymen, being pressed by hunger, took an opportunity, when they thought no one saw them, of trying to get a little privately; but they were discovered, and the attempt procured them some very severe floggings. One day, when we had a smooth sea and moderate wind, two of my wearied countrymen who were chained together (I was near them at the time), preferring death to such a life of misery, somehow made through the nettings and jumped into the sea: immediately another quite dejected fellow, who, on one account of his illness, was suffered to be out of irons, also followed their example; and I believe many more would very soon have done the same if they had not been prevented by the ship's crew, who were instantly alarmed. Those of us that were the most active were in a moment put down under the deck, and here was such a noise and confusion amongst the people of the ship as I never heard before, to stop her, and get the boat out to go after the slaves. However two of the wretches were drowned, but they got the other, and afterwards flogged him unmercifully for thus attempting to prefer death to slavery.

Journey to America

In this manner we continued to undergo more hardships than I can now relate, hardships which are inseparable from this accursed trade. Many a time we were near suffocation from the want of fresh air, which we were often without for whole days together. This, and the stench of the necessary tubs, carried off many. During our passage I first saw flying fishes, which surprised me very much: they used frequently to fly across the ship, and many of them fell on the deck. I also now first saw the use of the quadrant; I had often with astonishment seen the mariners make observations with it, and I could not think what it meant. They at last took notice of my surprise; and one of them, willing to increase it, as well as to gratify my curiosity, made me one day look through it. The clouds appeared to me to be land, which disappeared as they passed along. This heightened my wonder; and I was now more persuaded than ever that I was in another world, and that every thing about me was magic.

Arriving in America

At last we came in sight of the island of Barbadoes, at which the whites on board gave a great shout, and made many signs of joy to us. We did not know what to think of this; but as the vessel drew nearer we plainly saw the harbour, and other ships of different kinds and sizes; and we soon anchored amongst them off Bridge Town. Many merchants and planters now came on board, though it was in the evening. They put us in separate parcels, and examined us attentively. They also made us jump, and pointed to the land, signifying we were to go there. We thought by this we should be eaten by these ugly men, as they appeared to us; and, when soon after we were all put down under the deck again, there was much dread and trembling among us, and nothing but bitter cries to be heard all the night from these apprehensions, insomuch that at last the white people got some old slaves from the land to pacify us. They told us we were not to be eaten, but to work, and were soon to go on land, where we should see many of our country people. This report eased us much; and sure enough, soon after we were landed, there came to us Africans of all languages. We were conducted immediately to the merchant's yard, where we were all pent up together like so many sheep in a fold, without regard to sex or age. As every object was new to me every thing I saw filled me with surprise. What struck me first was that the houses were built with stories, and in every other respect different from those in Africa: but I was still more astonished on seeing people on horseback. I did not know what this could mean; and indeed I thought these people were full of nothing but magical arts. While I was in this astonishment one of my fellow prisoners spoke to a countryman of his about the horses, who said they were the same kind they had in their country. I understood them, though they were from a distant part of Africa, and I thought it odd I had not seen any horses there; but afterwards, when I came to converse with different Africans, I found they had many horses amongst them, and much larger than those I then saw. We were not many days in the merchant's custody before we were sold after their usual manner, which is this:—On a signal given (as the beat of a drum), the buyers rush at once into the yard where the slaves are confined, and make choice of that parcel they like best. The noise and clamour with which this is attended, and the eagerness visible in the countenances of the buyers, serve not a little to increase the apprehensions of the terrified Africans, who may well be supposed to consider them as the ministers of that destruction to which they think themselves devoted. In this manner, without scruple, are relations and friends separated, most of them never to see each other again. I remember in the vessel in which I was brought over, in the men's apartment, there were several brothers, who, in the sale, were sold in different lots; and it was very moving on this occasion to see and hear their cries at parting. O, ye nominal Christians! might not an African ask you, learned you this from your God, who says unto you, Do unto all men as you would men should do unto you? Is it not enough that we are torn from our country and friends to toil for your luxury and lust of gain? Must every tender feeling be likewise sacrificed to your avarice? Are the dearest friends and relations, now rendered more dear by their separation from their kindred, still to be parted from each other, and thus prevented from cheering the gloom of slavery with the small comfort of being together and mingling their sufferings and sorrows? Why are parents to lose their children, brothers their sisters, or husbands their wives? Surely this is a new refinement in cruelty, which, while it has no advantage to atone for it, thus aggravates distress, and adds fresh horrors even to the wretchedness of slavery.

Slavery Violates the Will of God

David Walker

David Walker, who was born a free black in North Carolina in 1785, attained literacy as a child. Walker traveled extensively as a young man and eventually settled in Boston, where he became involved in that city's budding abolitionist movement. He worked for *Freedom's Journal*, the first black weekly newspaper published in the United States, and he frequently lectured against slavery at abolitionist rallies and on Boston's street corners. Walker's greatest contribution to the abolitionist movement was the publication of a pamphlet titled *David Walker's Appeal* in 1829. The *Appeal*, which was reprinted several times and widely distributed, was one of the first antislavery treatises authored by an African American to be published in the United States. This excerpt from that text illustrates the religious foundation of Walker's critique of American slavery. A year after his vitriolic text was published, Walker died under mysterious circumstances.

I will give here a very imperfect list of the cruelties inflicted on us by the enlightened Christians of America.— First, no trifling portion of them will beat us nearly to death, if they find us on our knees praying to God,—They hinder us from going to hear the word of God—they keep us sunk in ignorance, and will not let us learn to read the word of God, nor write—If they find us with a book of any description in our hand, they will beat us nearly to death—they are

David Walker, *David Walker's Appeal, in Four Articles*, edited by Charles M. Wiltse, New York: Hill and Wang, 1965.

so afraid we will learn to read, and enlighten our dark and benighted minds—They will not suffer us to meet together to worship the God who made us—they brand us with hot iron—they cram bolts of fire down our throats—they cut us as they do horses, bulls, or hogs—they crop our ears and sometimes cut off bits of our tongues—they chain and handcuff us, and while in that miserable and wretched condition, beat us with cow-hides and clubs—they keep us half naked and starve us sometimes nearly to death under their infernal whips or lashes (which some of them shall have enough of yet)—They put on us fifty-sixes and chains, and make us work in that cruel situation, and in sickness, under lashes to support them and their families.—They keep us three or four hundred feet under ground working in their mines, night and day to dig up gold and silver to enrich them and their children.—They keep us in the most death-like ignorance by keeping us from all source of information, and call us, who are free men and next to the Angels of God, their property!!!!!! They make us fight and murder each other, many of us being ignorant, not knowing any better.—They take us, (being ignorant,) and put us as drivers one over the other, and make us afflict each other as bad as they themselves afflict us—and to crown the whole of this catalogue of cruelties, they tell us that we the (blacks) are an inferior race of beings! incapable of self government!!—We would be injurious to society and ourselves, if tyrants should loose their unjust hold on us!!! That if we were free we would not work, but would live on plunder or theft!!!! that we are the meanest and laziest set of beings in the world!!!!! That they are obliged to keep us in bondage to do us good!!!!!!—That we are satisfied to rest in slavery to them and their children!!!!!!—That we ought not to be set free in America, but ought to be sent away to Africa!!!!!!!!!—That if we were set free in America, we would involve the country in a civil war, which assertion is altogether at variance with our feeling or design, for we ask them for nothing but the rights of man, viz. for them to set us free, and treat us like men, and there will be no danger, for we will love and respect them, and protect our country—but cannot conscientiously do these things until they treat us like men.

God Will Punish Slave Owners

How cunning slave-holders think they are!!!—How much like the king of Egypt who, after he saw plainly that God was determined to bring out his people, in spite of him and his, as powerful as they were. He was willing that Moses, Aaron and the Elders of Israel, but not all the people should go and serve the Lord. But God deceived him as he will Christian Americans, unless they are very cautious how they move. What would have become of the United States of America, was it not for those among the whites, who not in words barely, but in truth and in deed, love and fear the Lord?—Our Lord and Master said:—"[But] Whoso shall offend one of these little ones which believe in me, it were better for him that a millstone were hanged about his neck, and that he were drowned in the depth of the sea." But the Americans with this very threatening of the Lord's, not only beat his little ones among the Africans, but many of them they put to death or murder. Now the avaricious Americans, think that the Lord Jesus Christ will let them off, because his words are no more than the words of a man!!! In fact, many of them are so avaricious and ignorant, that they do not believe in our Lord and Saviour Jesus Christ. Tyrants may think they are so skillful in State affairs is the reason that the government is preserved. But I tell you, that this country would have been given up long ago, was it not for the lovers of the Lord. They are indeed, the salt of the earth. Remove the people of God among the whites, from this land of blood, and it will stand until they cleverly get out of the way.

I adopt the language of the Rev. Mr. S.E. Cornish, of New York, editor of the Rights of All, and say: "Any coloured man of common intelligence, who gives his countenance and influence to that colony, further than its missionary object and interest extend, should be considered as a traitor to his brethren, and discarded by every respectable man of colour. And every member of that society, however pure his motive, whatever may be his religious character and moral worth, should in his efforts to remove the coloured population from their rightful soil, the land of their birth and nativity, be considered as acting gratuitously unrighteous and cruel."

Let me make an appeal brethren, to your hearts, for your cordial co-operation in the circulation of "The Rights of All," among us. The utility of such a vehicle conducted, cannot be estimated. I hope that the well informed among us, may see the absolute necessity of their co-operation in its universal spread among us. If we should let it go down, never let us undertake any thing of the kind again, but give up at once and say that we are really so ignorant and wretched that we cannot do any thing at all!!—As far as I have seen the writings of its editor, I believe he is not seeking to fill his pockets with money, but has the welfare of his brethren truly at heart. Such men, brethren, ought to be supported by us. . . .

Slaves Are Respectable People

The Americans may say or do as they please, but they have to raise us from the condition of brutes to that of respectable men, and to make a national acknowledgement to us for the wrongs they have inflicted on us. As unexpected, strange, and wild as these propositions may to some appear, it is no less a fact, that unless they are complied with, the Americans of the United States, though they may for a little while escape, God will yet weigh them in a balance, and if they are not superior to other men, as they have represented themselves to be, he will give them wretchedness to their very heart's content.

And now brethren, having concluded these four Articles, I submit them, together with my Preamble, dedicated to the Lord, for your inspection, in language so very simple, that the most ignorant, who can read at all, may easily understand—of which you may make the best you possibly can. Should tyrants take it into their heads to emancipate any of you, remember that your freedom is your natural right. You are men, as well as they, and instead of returning thanks to them for your freedom, return it to the Holy Ghost, who is our rightful owner. If they do not want to part with your labours, which have enriched them, let them keep you, and my word for it, that God Almighty, will break their strong band. Do you believe this, my brethren?—See my Address, delivered before the General Coloured Association of Massachusetts, which may be found in Freedom's Journal, for Dec. 20, 1828.—See the last clause of that Address. Whether you believe it or not, I tell you that God will dash tyrants, in combination with devils, into atoms, and will bring you out from your wretchedness and miseries under these *Christian People!!!!!!*

Those philanthropists and lovers of the human family, who have volunteered their services for our redemption from wretchedness, have a high claim on our gratitude, and we should always view them as our greatest earthly benefactors.

If any are anxious to ascertain who I am, know the world, that I am one of the oppressed, degraded and wretched sons of Africa, rendered so by the avaricious and unmerciful, among the whites.—If any wish to plunge me into the wretched incapacity of a slave, or murder me for the truth, know ye, that I am in the hand of God, and at your disposal. I count my life not dear unto me, but I am ready to be offered at any moment. For what is the use of living, when in fact I am dead. But remember, Americans, that as miserable, wretched, degraded and abject as you have made us in preceding, and in this generation, to support you and your families, that some of you (whites), on the continent of America, will yet curse the day that you ever were born. You want slaves, and want us for your slaves!!! My colour will yet, root some of you out of the very face of the earth!!!!!! You may doubt it if you please. I know that thousands will doubt—they think they have us so well secured in wretchedness, to them and their children, that it is impossible for such things to occur. So did the antideluvians doubt Noah, until the day in which the flood came and swept them away. So did the Sodomites doubt, until Lot had got out of the city, and God rained down fire and brimstone from Heaven upon them, and burnt them up. So did the king of Egypt doubt the very existence of a God; he said, "who is the Lord, that I should let Israel go?" Did he not find to his sorrow, who the Lord was, when he and all his mighty men of war, were smothered to death in the Red Sea? So did the Romans doubt, many of them were really so ignorant, that they thought the whole of mankind were made to be slaves to them; just as many of the Americans think now, of my colour. But they got dreadfully deceived. When men got their eyes opened, they made the murderers scamper. The way in which they cut their tyrannical throats, was not much inferior to the way the Romans or murderers, served them, when they held them in wretchedness and degradation under their feet. So would Christian Americans doubt, if God should send an Angel from Heaven to preach their funeral sermon. The fact is, the Christians having a name to live, while they are dead, think that God will screen them on that ground.

See the hundreds and thousands of us that are thrown into the seas by Christians, and murdered by them in other ways. They cram us into their vessel holds in chains and in hand-cuffs—men, women and children, all together!! O! save us, we pray thee, thou God of Heaven and of earth, from the devouring hands of the white Christians!!! . . .

In conclusion, I ask the candid and unprejudiced of the whole world, to search the pages of historians diligently, and see if the Antideluvians—the Sodomites—the Egyptians—the Babylonians—the Ninevites—the Carthagenians—the Persians—the Macedonians—the Greeks—the Romans—the Mahometans—the Jews—or devils, ever treated a set of human beings, as the white Christians of America do us, the blacks, or Africans. I also ask the attention of the world of mankind to the declaration of these very American people, of the United States.

A Slave Rebellion

Nat Turner

Nat Turner was a Virginia slave who wanted to abolish slavery through an armed rebellion against slaveholders. Claiming that God had spoken directly to him and ordered an attack on slave owners, Turner recruited more than sixty of his fellow slaves in his enterprise. Shortly after midnight on August 22, 1831, Turner and his followers launched their attack, killing some sixty whites—slave owners and their family members, including children and infants. Turner was eventually captured, tried, and executed for his actions. Before his execution, he narrated *The Confessions of Nat Turner* to Thomas R. Gray, an attorney. After Turner's death, Gray published the narrative. This excerpt from that text reveals how Turner came to initiate his rebellion and how he carried out his grisly work.

As I was praying one day at my plough, the spirit spoke to me, saying "Seek ye the kingdom of Heaven and all things shall be added unto you.["] . . .

After this revelation in the year 1825, and the knowledge of the elements being made known to me, I sought more than ever to obtain true holiness before the great day of judgment should appear, and then I began to receive the true knowledge of faith. And from the first steps of righteousness until the last, was I made perfect; and the Holy Ghost was with me, and said, "Behold me as I stand in the Heavens"— and I looked and saw the forms of men in different attitudes—and there were lights in the sky to which the chil-

Nat Turner, *The Confessions of Nat Turner and Related Documents*, edited by Kenneth S. Greenberg, Boston: Bedford Books of St. Martin's Press, 1996.

dren of darkness gave other names than what they really
were—for they were the lights of the Saviour's hands,
stretched forth from east to west, even as they were ex-
tended on the cross on Calvary for the redemption of sinners. And I wondered greatly at these miracles, and prayed
to be informed of a certainty of the meaning thereof—and
shortly afterwards, while laboring in the field, I discovered
drops of blood on the corn as though it were dew from
heaven—and I communicated it to many, both white and
black, in the neighborhood—and I then found on the leaves
in the woods hieroglyphic characters, and numbers, with the
forms of men in different attitudes, portrayed in blood, and
representing the figures I had seen before in the heavens.
And now the Holy Ghost had revealed itself to me, and
made plain the miracles it had shown me—For as the blood
of Christ had been shed on this earth, and had ascended to
heaven for the salvation of sinners, and was now returning
to earth again in the form of dew—and as the leaves on the
trees bore the impression of the figures I had seen in the
heavens, it was plain to me that the Saviour was about to lay
down the yoke he had borne for the sins of men, and the
great day of judgment was at hand.

Signs from Heaven

About this time I told these things to a white man (Etheldred
T. Brantley), on whom it had a wonderful effect—and he
ceased from his wickedness, and was attacked immediately
with a cutaneous eruption, and blood o[o]zed from the pores
of his skin, and after praying and fasting nine days, he was
healed, and the Spirit appeared to me again, and said, as the
Saviour had been baptised so should we be also—and when
the white people would not let us be baptised by the church,
we went down into the water together, in the sight of many
who reviled us, and were baptised by the Spirit—After this
I rejoiced greatly, and gave thanks to God. And on the 12th
of May, 1828, I heard a loud noise in the heavens, and the
Spirit instantly appeared to me and said the Serpent was
loosened, and Christ had laid down the yoke he had borne

for the sins of men, and that I should take it on and fight against the Serpent, for the time was fast approaching when the first should be last and the last should be first. . . .

And by signs in the heavens that it would make known to me when I should commence the great work—and until the first sign appeared, I should conceal it from the knowledge of men—And on the appearance of the sign (the eclipse of the sun last February), I should arise and prepare myself, and slay my enemies with their own weapons. And immediately on the sign appearing in the heavens, the seal was removed from my lips, and I communicated the great work laid out for me to do, to four in whom I had the greatest confidence. (Henry, Hark, Nelson, and Sam)—It was intended by us to have begun the work of death on the 4th July last— Many were the plans formed and rejected by us, and it affected my mind to such a degree, that I fell sick, and the time passed without our coming to any determination how to commence—Still forming new schemes and rejecting them, when the sign appeared again, which determined me not to wait longer.

Since the commencement of 1830, I had been living with Mr. Joseph Travis, who was to me a kind master, and placed the greatest confidence in me; in fact, I had no cause to complain of his treatment to me. On Saturday evening, the 20th of August, it was agreed between Henry, Hark and myself, to prepare a dinner the next day for the men we expected, and then to concert a plan, as we had not yet determined on any. Hark, on the following morning, brought a pig, and Henry brandy, and being joined by Sam, Nelson, Will and Jack, they prepared in the woods a dinner, where, about three o'clock, I joined them. . . .

The Rebellion Begins

I saluted them on coming up, and asked Will how came he there, he answered, his life was worth no more than others, and his liberty as dear to him. I asked him if he thought to obtain it? He said he would, or lose his life. This was enough to put him in full confidence. Jack, I knew, was only a tool

in the hands of Hark, it was quickly agreed we should commence at home (Mr. J. Travis') on that night, and until we
had armed and equipped ourselves, and gathered sufficient
force, neither age nor sex was to be spared, (which was in-
variably adhered to). We remained at the feast, until about
two hours in the night, when we went to the house and found
Austin; they all went to the cider press and drank, except
myself. On returning to the house, Hark went to the door
with an axe, for the purpose of breaking it open, as we knew
we were strong enough to murder the family, if they were
awaked by the noise; but reflecting that it might create an
alarm in the neighborhood, we determined to enter the house
secretly, and murder them whilst sleeping. Hark got a ladder
and set it against the chimney, on which I ascended, and
hoisting a window, entered and came down stairs, unbarred
the door, and removed the guns from their places. It was then
observed that I must spill the first blood. On which, armed
with a hatchet, and accompanied by Will, I entered my master's chamber, it being dark, I could not give a death blow,
the hatchet glanced from his head, he sprang from the bed
and called his wife, it was his last word, Will laid him dead,
with a blow of his axe, and Mrs. Travis shared the same fate,
as she lay in bed. The murder of this family, five in number,
was the work of a moment, not one of them awoke; there
was a little infant sleeping in a cradle, that was forgotten, until we had left the house and gone some distance, when
Henry and Will returned and killed it; we got here, four guns
that would shoot, and several old muskets, with a pound or
two of powder. We remained some time at the barn, where
we paraded; I formed them in a line as soldiers, and after
carrying them through all the manœuvres I was master of,
marched them off to Mr. Salathul Francis', about six hundred yards distant. Sam and Will went to the door and
knocked. Mr. Francis asked who was there, Sam replied it
was him, and he had a letter for him, on which he got up and
came to the door; they immediately seized him, and drag-
ging him out a little from the door, he was dispatched by repeated blows on the head; there was no other white person

in the family. We started from there for Mrs. Reese's, maintaining the most perfect silence on our march, where finding the door unlocked, we entered, and murdured Mrs. Reese in her bed, while sleeping; her son awoke, but it was only to sleep the sleep of death, he had only time to say who is that, and he was no more. From Mrs. Reese's we went to Mrs. Turner's, a mile distant, which we reached about sunrise, on Monday morning. Henry, Austin, and Sam, went to the still, where, finding Mr. Peebles, Austin shot him, and the rest of us went to the house; as we approached, the family discovered us, and shut the door. Vain hope! Will, with one stroke of his axe, opened it, and we entered and found Mrs. Turner and Mrs. Newsome in the middle of a room, almost frightened to death. Will immediately killed Mrs. Turner, with one blow of his axe. I took Mrs. Newsome by the hand, and with the sword I had when I was apprehended, I struck her several blows over the head, but not being able to kill her, as the sword was dull. Will turning around and discovering it, despatched her also. A general destruction of property and search for money and ammunition, always succeeded the murders. By this time my company amounted to fifteen, and nine men mounted, who started for Mrs. Whitehead's (the other six were to go through a by way to Mr. Bryant's, and rejoin us at Mrs. Whitehead's), as we approached the house we discovered Mr. Richard Whitehead standing in the cotton patch, near the lane fence; we called him over into the lane, and Will, the executioner, was near at hand, with his fatal axe, to send him to an untimely grave. As we pushed on to the house, I discovered some one run round the garden, and thinking it was some of the white family, I pursued them, but finding it was a servant girl belonging to the house, I returned to commence the work of death, but they whom I left, had not been idle; all the family were already murdered, but Mrs. Whitehead and her daughter Margaret. As I came round to the door I saw Will pulling Mrs. Whitehead out of the house, and at the step he nearly severed her head from her body, with his broad axe. Miss Margaret, when I discovered her, had concealed herself in the corner, formed by the projection of the cellar cap from the house; on my approach she fled, but was soon overtaken, and after repeated blows with a sword, I killed her by a blow on the head, with a fence rail. By this time, the six who had gone by Mr. Bryant's, rejoined us, and informed me they had done the work of death assigned them. We again divided, part going to Mr. Richard Porter's, and from thence to Nathaniel Francis', the others to Mr. Howell Harris', and Mr. T. Doyles. On my reaching Mr. Porter's, he had escaped with his family. I understood there, that the alarm had already spread, and I immediately returned to bring up those sent to Mr. Doyles, and Mr. Howell Harris'; the party I left going on to Mr. Francis', having told them I would join them in that neighborhood. I met these sent to Mr. Doyles' and Mr. Harris' returning, having met Mr. Doyle on the road and killed him; and learning from some who joined them, that Mr. Harris was from home, I immediately pursued the course taken by the party gone on before; but knowing they would complete the work of death and pillage, at Mr. Francis' before I could get there, I went to Mr. Peter Edwards', expecting to find them there, but they had been here also. I then went to Mr. John T. Barrow's, they had been here and murdered him. I pursued on their track to Capt. Newit Harris', where I found the greater part mounted, and ready to start; the men now amounting to about forty, shouted and hurraed as I rode up, some were in the yard, loading their guns, others drinking. They said Captain Harris and his family had escaped, the property in the house they destroyed, robbing him of money and other valuables. I ordered them to mount and march instantly, this was about nine or ten o'clock, Monday morning. I proceeded to Mr. Levi Waller's, two or three miles distant. I took my station in the rear, and as it 'twas my object to carry terror and devastation wherever we went, I placed fifteen or twenty of the best armed and most to be relied on, in front, who generally approached the house as fast as their horses could run; this was for two purposes, to prevent their escape and strike terror to the inhabitants—on this account I never got to the houses, after leaving Mrs. Whitehead's, until the murders were committed, except in one case. I sometimes got in sight in time to see the work of death completed, viewed the mangled bodies as they lay, in silent satisfaction, and immediately started in quest of other victims—Having murdered Mrs. Waller and ten children, we started for Mr. William Williams'—having killed him and two little boys that were there; while engaged in this, Mrs. Williams fled and got some distance from the house, but she was pursued, overtaken, and compelled to get up behind one of the company, who brought her back, and after showing her the mangled body of her lifeless husband, she was told to get down and lay by his side, where she was shot dead. I then started for Mr. Jacob Williams, where the family were murdered—Here we found a young man named Drury, who had come on business with Mr. Williams—he was pursued, overtaken and shot. Mrs. Vaughan was the next place we visited—and after murdering the family here, I determined on starting for Jerusalem.

The Rebellion Spreads

Our number amounted now to fifty or sixty, all mounted and armed with guns, axes, swords and clubs—On reaching Mr. James W. Parkers' gate, immediately on the road leading to Jerusalem, and about three miles distant, it was proposed to me to call there, but I objected, as I knew he was gone to Jerusalem, and my object was to reach there as soon as possible; but some of the men having relations at Mr. Parker's it was agreed that they might call and get his people. I remained at the gate on the road, with seven or eight; the others going across the field to the house, about half a mile off. After waiting some time for them, I became impatient, and started to the house for them, and on our return we were met by a party of white men, who had pursued our blood-stained track, and who had fired on those at the gate, and dispersed them, which I new nothing of, not having been at that time rejoined by any of them—Immediately on discovering the whites, I ordered my men to halt and form, as they appeared to be alarmed—The white men, eighteen in number, approached us in about one hundred yards, when one of them fired (this was against the positive orders of Captain Alexander P. Peete, who commanded, and who had directed the men to reserve their fire until within thirty paces). And I discovered about half of them retreating, I then ordered my men to fire and rush on them; the few remaining stood their ground until we approached within fifty yards, when they fired and retreated. We pursued and overtook some of them who we thought we left dead (they were not killed); after pursuing them about two hundred yards, and rising a little hill, I discovered they were met by another party, and had haulted, and were re-loading their guns (this was a small party from Jerusalem who knew the negroes were in the field, and had just tied their horses to await their return to the road, knowing that Mr. Parker and family were in Jerusalem, but knew nothing of the party that had gone in with Captain Peete; on hearing the firing they immediately rushed to the spot and arrived just in time to arrest the progress of these barbarous villians, and save the lives of their friends and fellow citizens). Thinking that those who retreated first, and the party who fired on us at fifty or sixty yards distant, had all only fallen back to meet others with amunition.

The Rebellion Is Broken

As I saw them re-loading their guns, and more coming up than I saw at first, and several of my bravest men being wounded, the others became panick struck and squandered over the field; the white men pursued and fired on us several times. Hark had his horse shot under him, and I caught another for him as it was running by me; five or six of my men were wounded, but none left on the field; finding myself defeated here I instantly determined to go through a private way, and cross the Nottoway river at the Cypress Bridge, three miles below Jerusalem, and attack that place in the rear, as I expected they would look for me on the other road, and I had a great desire to get there to procure arms and amunition. After going a short distance in this private way, accompanied by about twenty men, I overtook two or three who told me the others were dispersed in every direction. After tyring [sic] in vain to collect a sufficient force to proceed to Jerusalem, I determined to return, as I was sure they would make back to their old neighborhood, where they would rejoin me, make new recruits, and come down again. On my way back, I called at Mrs. Thomas's, Mrs. Spencer's, and several other places, the white families having fled, we found no more victims to gratify our thirst for blood, we stopped at Majr. Ridley's quarter for the night, and being joined by four of his men, with the recruits made since my defeat, we mustered now about forty strong. After placing out sentinels, I laid down to sleep, but was quickly roused by a great racket; starting up, I found some mounted, and others in great confusion; one of the sentinels having given the alarm that we were about to be attacked, I ordered some to ride round and reconnoitre, and on their return the others being more alarmed, not knowing who they were, fled in different ways, so that I was reduced to about twenty again; with this I determined to attempt to recruit, and proceed on to rally in the neighborhood, I had left. Dr. Blunt's was the nearest house, which we reached just before day; on riding up the yard, Hark fired a gun. We expected Dr. Blunt and his family were at Maj. Ridley's, as I knew there was a company of men there; the gun was fired to ascertain if any of the family were at home; we were immediately fired upon and retreated, leaving several of my men. I do not know what became of them, as I never saw them afterwards. Pursuing our course back and coming in sight of Captain Harris', where we had been the day before, we discovered a party of white men at the house, on which all deserted me but two (Jacob and Nat), we concealed ourselves in the woods until near night, when I sent them in search of Henry, Sam, Nelson, and Hark, and directed them to rally all they could, at the place we had had our dinner the Sunday before, where they would find me, and I accordingly returned there as soon as it was dark and remained until Wednesday evening, when discovering white men riding around the place as though they were looking for some one, and none of my men joining me, I concluded Jacob and Nat had been taken, and compelled to betray me. On this I gave up all hope for the present; and on Thursday night after having supplied myself with provisions from Mr. Travis's, I scratched a hole under a pile of fence rails in a field, where I concealed myself for six weeks, never leaving my hiding place but for a few minutes in the dead of night to get water which was very near; thinking by this time I could venture out, I began to go about in the night and eaves drop the houses in the neighborhood; pursuing this course for about a fortnight and gathering little or no intelligence, afraid of speaking to any human being, and returning every morning to my cave before the dawn of day.

Captured

I know not how long I might have led this life, if accident had not betrayed me, a dog in the neighborhood passing by my hiding place one night while I was out, was attracted by some meat I had in my cave, and crawled in and stole it, and was coming out just as I returned. A few nights after, two negroes having started to go hunting with the same dog, and passed that way, the dog came again to the place, and having just gone out to walk about, discovered me and barked, on which thinking myself discovered, I spoke to them to beg concealment. On making myself known they fled from me. Knowing then they would betray me, I immediately left my hiding place, and was pursued almost incessantly until I was taken a fortnight afterwards by Mr. Benjamin Phipps, in a little hole I had dug out with my sword, for the purpose of concealment, under the top of a fallen tree. On Mr. Phipps' discovering the place of my concealment, he cocked his gun and aimed at me. I requested him not to shoot and I would give up, upon which he demanded my sword. I delivered it to him, and he brought me to prison. During the time I was pursued, I had many hair breadth escapes, which your time will not permit you to relate. I am here loaded with chains, and willing to suffer the fate that awaits me.

Becoming an Abolitionist Leader

Frederick Douglass

Frederick Douglass was born a slave in Maryland in around
1818. At the age of twenty, he escaped from his master and
fled to the North. A few years later, Douglass commenced a
remarkable public career that made him the most influential
black leader and reformer of the nineteenth century. A self-
taught reader and writer, Douglass began his public career as
an abolitionist orator and journalist. He spoke at abolitionist
conventions and contributed articles to *The Liberator* and
other abolitionist newspapers. In 1845, he published his first
of three autobiographies, *Narrative of the Life of Frederick
Douglass, an American Slave*, which is considered by many
literary historians as the greatest American slave narrative. In
1847, Douglass established *The North Star*, the first of three
abolitionist newspapers that he edited. During the Civil War,
Douglass continued to urge both the abolition of slavery and
the recruitment of African American troops for the Union
army. After the war, he became involved with a number of
reform movements, promoting civil rights, the elective franchise for black Americans, and women's suffrage. This passage from Douglass's second autobiography, *My Bondage
and My Freedom*, published in 1855, explains how he became
involved with the abolitionist movement.

In the summer of 1841, a grand anti-slavery convention
was held in Nantucket, under the auspices of [white-

Frederick Douglass, *My Bondage and My Freedom*, edited by William L. Andrews, Urbana:
University of Illinois Press, 1987.

antislavery activist] Mr. [William Lloyd] Garrison and his friends. Until now, I had taken no holiday since my escape from slavery. Having worked very hard that spring and summer, in Richmond's brass foundery—sometimes working all night as well as all day—and needing a day or two of rest, I attended this convention, never supposing that I should take part in the proceedings. Indeed, I was not aware that any one connected with the convention even so much as knew my name. I was, however, quite mistaken. Mr. William C. Coffin, a prominent abolitionist in those days of trial, had heard me speaking to my colored friends, in the little schoolhouse on Second street, New Bedford, where we worshiped. He sought me out in the crowd, and invited me to say a few words to the convention. Thus sought out, and thus invited, I was induced to speak out the feelings inspired by the occasion, and the fresh recollection of the scenes through which I had passed as a slave. My speech on this occasion is about the only one I ever made, of which I do not remember a single connected sentence. It was with the utmost difficulty that I could stand erect, or that I could command and articulate two words without hesitation and stammering. I trembled in every limb. I am not sure that my embarrassment was not the most effective part of my speech, if speech it could be called. At any rate, this is about the only part of my performance that I now distinctly remember. But excited and convulsed as I was, the audience, though remarkably quiet before, became as much excited as myself. Mr. Garrison followed me, taking me as his text; and now, whether I had made an eloquent speech in behalf of freedom or not, his was one never to be forgotten by those who heard it. Those who had heard Mr. Garrison oftenest, and had known him longest, were astonished. It was an effort of unequaled power, sweeping down, like a very tornado, every opposing barrier, whether of sentiment or opinion. For a moment, he possessed that almost fabulous inspiration, often referred to but seldom attained, in which a public meeting is transformed, as it were, into a single individuality—the orator wielding a thousand heads and hearts at once, and by the simple majesty of his all controlling thought, converting his hearers into the express image of his own soul. That night there were at least one thousand Garrisonians in Nantucket! At the close of this great meeting, I was duly waited on by Mr. John A. Collins—then the general agent of the Massachusetts anti-slavery society—and urgently solicited by him to become an agent of that society, and to publicly advocate its anti-slavery principles. I was reluctant to take the proffered position. I had not been quite three years from slavery—was honestly distrustful of my ability—wished to be excused; publicity exposed me to discovery and arrest by my master; and other objections came up, but Mr. Collins was not to be put off, and I finally consented to go out for three months, for I supposed that I should have got to the end of my story and my usefulness, in that length of time.

A New Life

Here, opened upon me a new life—a life for which I had had no preparation. I was a "graduate from the peculiar institution," Mr. Collins used to say, when introducing me, *"with my diploma written on my back!"* The three years of my freedom had been spent in the hard school of adversity. My hands had been furnished by nature with something like a solid leather coating, and I had bravely marked out for myself a life of rough labor, suited to the hardness of my hands, as a means of supporting myself and rearing my children.

Now what shall I say of this fourteen years' experience as a public advocate of the cause of my enslaved brothers and sisters? The time is but as a speck, yet large enough to justify a pause for retrospection—and a pause it must only be.

Young, ardent, and hopeful, I entered upon this new life in the full gush of unsuspecting enthusiasm. The cause was good; the men engaged in it were good; the means to attain its triumph, good; Heaven's blessing must attend all, and freedom must soon be given to the pining millions under a ruthless bondage. My whole heart went with the holy cause, and my most fervent prayer to the Almighty Disposer of the hearts of men, were continually offered for its early triumph.

"Who or what," thought I, "can withstand a cause so good, so holy, so indescribably glorious. The God of Israel is with us. The might of the Eternal is on our side. Now let but the truth be spoken, and a nation will start forth at the sound!" In this enthusiastic spirit, I dropped into the ranks of freedom's friends, and went forth to the battle. For a time I was made to forget that my skin was dark and my hair crisped. For a time I regretted that I could not have shared the hardships and dangers endured by the earlier workers for the slave's release. I soon, however, found that my enthusiasm had been extravagant; that hardships and dangers were not

---

Saving the Union Requires the Abolition of Slavery

During the Civil War, Frederick Douglass continued to demand the abolition of slavery. In this excerpt from a speech delivered in Rochester, New York, on March 25, 1862, Douglass argues that saving the Union necessitates the abolition of slavery.

In the tremendous conflict through which we are now passing, all events steadily conspire, to make the cause of the slave and the cause of the country identical. He who to-day fights for Emancipation, fights for his country and free Institutions, and he who fights for slavery, fights against his country and in favor of a slaveholding oligarchy.

This was always so, though only abolitionists perceived the fact. The difference between them and others is this: They got an earlier glimpse at the black heart of slavery—than others did. They saw in times of seeming peace, for the peace we had, was only seeming—what we can only see in times of open war. They saw that a nation like ours, containing two such opposite forces as liberty and slavery, could not enjoy permanent peace, and they said so and got mobbed for saying so.

Frederick Douglass, *Selected Speeches and Writings.* Ed. by Philip S. Foner. Chicago: Lawrence Hill Books, 1999, pp. 486–87.

yet passed; and that the life now before me, had shadows as well as sunbeams.

Among the first duties assigned me, on entering the ranks, was to travel, in company with Mr. George Foster, to secure subscribers to the "Anti-slavery Standard" and the "Liberator." With him I traveled and lectured through the eastern counties of Massachusetts. Much interest was awakened— large meetings assembled. Many came, no doubt, from curiosity to hear what a negro could say in his own cause. I was generally introduced as a *"chattel"*—a *"thing"*—a piece of southern *"property"*—the chairman assuring the audience that *it* could speak. Fugitive slaves, at that time, were not so plentiful as now; and as a fugitive slave lecturer, I had the advantage of being a *"brand new fact"*—the first one out. Up to that time, a colored man was deemed a fool who confessed himself a runaway slave, not only because of the danger to which he exposed himself of being retaken, but because it was a confession of a very *low* origin! Some of my colored friends in New Bedford thought very badly of my wisdom for thus exposing and degrading myself. The only precaution I took, at the beginning, to prevent Master Thomas from knowing where I was, and what I was about, was the withholding my former name, my master's name, and the name of the state and county from which I came. During the first three or four months, my speeches were almost exclusively made up of narrations of my own personal experience as a slave. "Let us have the facts," said the people. So also said Friend George Foster, who always wished to pin me down to my simple narrative. "Give us the facts," said Collins, "we will take care of the philosophy." Just here arose some embarrassment. It was impossible for me to repeat the same old story month after month, and to keep up my interest in it. It was new to the people, it is true, but it was an old story to me; and to go through with it night after night, was a task altogether too mechanical for my nature. "Tell your story, Frederick," would whisper my then revered friend, William Lloyd Garrison, as I stepped upon the platform. I could not always obey, for I was now reading and thinking. New views of the subject were presented to my mind. It did not entirely satisfy me to *narrate* wrongs; I felt like *denouncing* them. I could not always curb my moral indignation for the perpetrators of slaveholding villainy, long enough for a circumstantial statement of the facts which I felt almost everybody must know. Besides, I was growing, and needed room. "People won't believe you ever was a slave, Frederick, if you keep on this way," said Friend Foster. "Be yourself," said Collins, "and tell your story." It was said to me, "Better have a *little* of the plantation manner of speech than not; 'tis not best that you seem too learned." These excellent friends were actuated by the best of motives, and were not altogether wrong in their advice; and still I must speak just the word that seemed to *me* the word to be spoken *by* me.

Confronting the Doubters

At last the apprehended trouble came. People doubted if I had ever been a slave. They said I did not talk like a slave, look like a slave, nor act like a slave, and that they believed I had never been south of Mason and Dixon's line. "He don't tell us where he came from—what his master's name was—how he got away—nor the story of his experience. Besides, he is educated, and is, in this, a contradiction of all the facts we have concerning the ignorance of the slaves." Thus, I was in a pretty fair way to be denounced as an impostor. The committee of the Massachusetts anti-slavery society knew all the facts in my case, and agreed with me in the prudence of keeping them private. They, therefore, never doubted my being a genuine fugitive; but going down the aisles of the churches in which I spoke, and hearing the free spoken Yankees saying, repeatedly, *"He's never been a slave, I'll warrent ye,"* I resolved to dispel all doubt, at no distant day, by such a revelation of facts as could not be made by any other than a genuine fugitive.

In a little less than four years, therefore, after becoming a public lecturer, I was induced to write out the leading facts connected with my experience in slavery, giving names of persons, places, and dates—thus putting it in the power of any who doubted, to ascertain the truth or falsehood of my story of being a fugitive slave. This statement soon became known in Maryland, and I had reason to believe that an effort would be made to recapture me.

It is not probable that any open attempt to secure me as a slave could have succeeded, further than the obtainment, by my master, of the money value of my bones and sinews. Fortunately for me, in the four years of my labors in the abolition cause, I had gained many friends, who would have suffered themselves to be taxed to almost any extent to save me from slavery. It was felt that I had committed the double offense of running away, and exposing the secrets and crimes of slavery and slaveholders. There was a double motive for seeking my reenslavement—avarice and vengeance; and while, as I have said, there was little probability of successful recapture, if attempted openly, I was constantly in danger of being spirited away, at a moment when my friends could render me no assistance. In traveling about from place to place—often alone—I was much exposed to this sort of attack. Any one cherishing the design to betray me, could easily do so, by simply tracing my whereabouts through the anti-slavery journals, for my meetings and movements were promptly made known in advance. My true friends, Mr. Garrison and Mr. Phillips, had no faith in the power of Massachusetts to protect me in my right to liberty. Public sentiment and the law, in their opinion, would hand me over to the tormentors. Mr. Phillips, especially, considered me in danger, and said, when I showed him the manuscript of my story, if in my place, he would throw it into the fire. Thus, the reader will observe, the settling of one difficulty only opened the way for another; and that though I had reached a free state, and had attained a position for public usefulness, I was still tormented with the liability of losing my liberty.

A Woman Abolitionist Speaks Out

Sojourner Truth

> Sojourner Truth was born a slave in New York in around
> 1797. She was named Isabella at birth, but she changed her
> name when she became free—by state law—in 1828. During
> the 1840s, Truth began lecturing at religious camp meetings
> on the evils of slavery. In 1850, Truth, who never attained lit-
> eracy, dictated her life story to Olive Gilbert, a white aboli-
> tionist, who published the account as *Narrative of Sojourner
> Truth*. During the 1850s, Truth earned a national reputation as
> an antislavery and women's rights activist and orator. Her
> fame resulted in a meeting with President Abraham Lincoln
> in 1864, during which Truth and Lincoln discussed civil
> rights for the newly freed slaves. In 1878, Gilbert published
> an updated version of Truth's *Narrative*. This excerpt from
> that text captures Truth addressing a women's rights conven-
> tion in Akron, Ohio, in 1851. The episode, narrated by
> Frances D. Gage, who chaired the meeting, suggests the diffi-
> culty that black abolitionists encountered when they delivered
> their message, even to the progressive thinkers assembled at a
> women's rights convention.

In the year 1851 she [Sojourner Truth] left her home in
Northampton, Mass., for a lecturing tour in Western New
York, accompanied by the Hon. George Thompson of En-

Sojourner Truth, *Narrative of Sojourner Truth*, edited by Ernest Kaiser, New York: Arno
Press, 1968.

gland, and other distinguished abolitionists. To advocate the cause of the enslaved at this period was both unpopular and unsafe. Their meetings were frequently disturbed or broken up by the pro-slavery mob, and their lives imperiled. At such times, Sojourner fearlessly maintained her ground, and by her dignified manner and opportune remarks would disperse the rabble and restore order.

She spent several months in Western New York, making Rochester her head-quarters. Leaving this State, she traveled westward, and the next glimpse we get of her is in a Woman's Rights Convention at Akron, Ohio. Mrs. Frances D. Gage, who presided at that meeting, relates the following:—

"The cause was unpopular then. The leaders of the movement trembled on seeing a tall, gaunt black woman, in a gray dress and white turban, surmounted by an uncouth sun-bonnet, march deliberately into the church, walk with the air of a queen up the aisle, and take her seat upon the pulpit steps. A buzz of disapprobation was heard all over the house, and such words as these fell upon listening ears:—

An Unwelcome Reception

"'An abolition affair!' 'Woman's rights and niggers!' 'We told you so!' 'Go it, old darkey!'

"I chanced upon that occasion to wear my first laurels in public life as president of the meeting. At my request, order was restored and the business of the hour went on. The morning session was held; the evening exercises came and went. Old Sojourner, quiet and reticent as the 'Libyan Statue,' sat crouched against the wall on the corner of the pulpit stairs, her sun-bonnet shading her eyes, her elbows on her knees, and her chin resting upon her broad, hard palm. At intermission she was busy, selling 'The Life of Sojourner Truth,' a narrative of her own strange and adventurous life. Again and again timorous and trembling ones came to me and said with earnestness, 'Do n't let her speak, Mrs. Gage, it will ruin us. Every newspaper in the land will have our cause mixed with abolition and niggers, and we shall be utterly denounced.' My only answer was, 'We shall see when the time comes.'

"The second day the work waxed warm. Methodist, Baptist, Episcopal, Presbyterian, and Universalist ministers came in to hear and discuss the resolutions presented. One claimed superior rights and privileges for man on the ground of superior intellect; another, because of the manhood of Christ. 'If God had desired the equality of woman, he would have given some token of his will through the birth, life, and death of the Saviour.' Another gave us a theological view of the sin of our first mother. There were few women in those days that dared to 'speak in meeting,' and the august teachers of the people were seeming to get the better of us, while the boys in the galleries and the sneerers among the pews were hugely enjoying the discomfiture, as they supposed, of the 'strong minded.' Some of the tender-skinned friends were on the point of losing dignity, and the atmosphere of the convention betokened a storm.

"Slowly from her seat in the corner rose Sojourner Truth, who, till now, had scarcely lifted her head. 'Do n't let her speak!' gasped half a dozen in my ear. She moved slowly and solemnly to the front, laid her old bonnet at her feet, and turned her great, speaking eyes to me. There was a hissing sound of disapprobation above and below. I rose and announced 'Sojourner Truth,' and begged the audience to keep silence for a few moments. The tumult subsided at once, and every eye was fixed on this almost Amazon form, which stood nearly six feet high, head erect, and eye piercing the upper air, like one in a dream. At her first word, there was a profound hush. She spoke in deep tones, which, though not loud, reached every ear in the house, and away through the throng at the doors and windows:—

Sojourner Truth Speaks

"'Well, chilern, whar dar is so much racket dar must be something out o' kilter. I tink dat 'twixt de niggers of de Souf and de women at de Norf all a talkin' 'bout rights, de white men will be in a fix pretty soon. But what's all dis here talkin' 'bout? Dat man ober dar say dat women needs to be helped into carriages, and lifted ober ditches, and to have de best place every whar. Nobody eber help me into carriages, or ober mud puddles, or gives me any best place [and raising herself to her full height and her voice to a pitch like rolling thunder, she asked], and ar'n't I a woman? Look at me! Look at my arm! [And she bared her right arm to the shoulder, showing her tremendous muscular power.] I have plowed, and planted, and gathered into barns, and no man could head me—and ar'n't I a woman? I could work as much and eat as much as a man (when I could get it), and bear de lash as well—and ar'n't I a woman? I have borne thirteen chilern and seen 'em mos' all sold off into slavery, and when I cried out with a mother's grief, none but Jesus heard—and ar'n't I a woman? Den dey talks 'bout dis ting in de head—what dis dey call it?' 'Intellect,' whispered some one near. 'Dat's it honey. What's dat got to do with women's rights or niggers' rights? If my cup won't hold but a pint and yourn holds a quart, would n't ye be mean not to let me have my little half-measure full?' And she pointed her significant finger and sent a keen glance at the minister who had made the argument. The cheering was long and loud.

"'Den dat little man in black dar, he say women can't have as much rights as man, cause Christ want a woman. Whar did your Christ come from?' Rolling thunder could not have stilled that crowd as did those deep, wonderful tones, as she stood there with outstretched arms and eye of fire. Raising her voice still louder, she repeated, 'Whar did your Christ come from? From God and a woman. Man had nothing to do with him.' Oh! what a rebuke she gave the little man.

"'Turning again to another objector, she took up the defense of mother Eve. I cannot follow her through it all. It was pointed, and witty, and solemn, eliciting at almost every sentence deafening applause; and she ended by asserting that 'if de fust woman God ever made was strong enough to turn the world upside down, all 'lone, dese togedder [and she glanced her eye over us], ought to be able to turn it back and get it right side up again, and now dey is asking to do it, de men better let em.' Long-continued cheering. 'Bleeged to ye for hearin' on me, and now ole Sojourner ha'n't got nothing more to say.'

Applause for the Former Slave

"Amid roars of applause, she turned to her corner, leaving more than one of us with streaming eyes and hearts beating with gratitude. She had taken us up in her strong arms and carried us safely over the slough of difficulty, turning the whole tide in our favor. I have never in my life seen anything like the magical influence that subdued the mobbish spirit of the day and turned the jibes and sneers of an excited crowd into notes of respect and admiration. Hundreds rushed up to shake hands, and congratulate the glorious old mother and bid her God speed on her mission of 'testifying again concerning the wickedness of this 'ere people.'"

Mrs. Gage also in the same article relates the folowing:—

"Once upon a Sabbath in Michigan an abolition meeting was held. Parker Pillsbury was speaker, and criticized freely the conduct of the churches regarding slavery. While he was speaking there came up a fearful thunder storm. A young Methodist arose, and interrupting the speaker, said he felt alarmed; he felt as if God's judgment was about to fall on him for daring to sit and hear such blasphemy; that it made his hair almost rise with terror. Here a voice, sounding above the rain that beat upon the roof, the sweeping surge of the winds, the crashing of the limbs of trees, the swaying of branches, and the rolling of thunder, spoke out: 'Chile, do n't be skeered; you are not going to be harmed. I do n't speck God's ever hearn tell on ye.' It was all she said, but it was enough."

Chapter 2

The Civil War and Reconstruction Eras

Chapter Preface

The abolitionists achieved their goal during the Civil War. On January 1, 1863, President Abraham Lincoln issued the Emancipation Proclamation, which freed the slaves in all states in rebellion against the Union. By the war's end, both houses of Congress had approved the Thirteenth Amendment to the U.S. Constitution, which prohibited slavery in the United States and its territories. But the Civil War and the Reconstruction period that followed it presented an array of political, social, and economic issues to be addressed by the African American leadership.

During the war, Frederick Douglass and other abolitionists urged President Lincoln to recruit black soldiers for the Union army. In desperate need of men to fight the war, Lincoln finally allowed blacks to enlist. The Emancipation Proclamation included a statement opening the Union army and navy to black recruits. Before the war's end, almost two hundred thousand African Americans enlisted, providing a fresh supply of manpower that helped turn the tide of the war in the North's favor.

When it became obvious that slavery would be a casualty of the war, African American reformers began to devote attention to the role that blacks would play in postwar American society. Would they enjoy all the rights of citizenship, such as the ability to vote and run for public office? How would they be educated? How would the 4 million former slaves earn their living?

The Reconstruction era became a time of great reforms for black Americans. The Constitution was twice amended in an attempt to grant African Americans full rights of citizenship. The Fourteenth Amendment, enacted in 1868, made blacks U.S. citizens and guaranteed them "equal protection of the laws." The Fifteenth Amendment, adopted in

1870, prohibited the United States or any state from denying citizens the right to vote "on account of race, color, or previous condition of servitude." In addition, Congress passed two Civil Rights Acts during Reconstruction, one in 1866 and one in 1875, that attempted to bestow citizenship rights to black Americans.

Assistance for the Newly Freed Slaves

Harriet Jacobs

> Harriet Jacobs was born a slave in North Carolina in 1813. At
> age twenty-one, she escaped from slavery and fled to the
> North, where she became acquainted with Amy Post, Harriet
> Beecher Stowe, and other prominent abolitionists. In 1861,
> Jacobs, using the pseudonym Linda Brent, published *Inci-
> dents in the Life of a Slave Girl*, the first slave narrative writ-
> ten by a woman. During the Civil War, Jacobs contributed
> articles to *The Liberator* and other abolitionist newspapers. In
> 1862, she traveled to Washington, D.C., to examine the living
> conditions of runaway slaves—referred to during the war as
> contraband. The following letter written to William Lloyd
> Garrison, the editor of *The Liberator*, on September 5, 1862,
> alerts the abolitionist leadership that something had to be
> done for refugee slaves displaced by the war. In the letter
> Jacobs highlights problems that would have to be addressed
> by African American reformers after emancipation—how the
> former slaves would be educated, where they would live, how
> they would earn a living.

Dear Mr. Garrison:

I thank you for the request of a line on the condition
of the contrabands, and what I have seen while among them.
When we parted at that pleasant gathering of the Progressive
Friends at Longwood, you to return to the Old Bay State
[Massachusetts], to battle for freedom and justice to the

Harriet Jacobs, "Life Among the Contrabands," *Incidents in the Life of a Slave Girl*, edited
by Nellie Y. McKay and Frances Smith Foster, New York: W.W. Norton, 2001.

slave, I to go to the District of Columbia, where the shackles had just fallen, I hoped that the glorious echo from the blow had aroused the spirit of freedom, if a spark slumbered in its bosom. Having purchased my ticket through to Washington at the Philadelphia station, I reached the capital without molestation. Next morning, I went to Duff Green's Row, Government head-quarters for the contrabands here. I found men, women and children all huddled together, without any distinction or regard to age or sex. Some of them were in the most pitiable condition. Many were sick with measles, diptheria, scarlet and typhoid fever. Some had a few filthy rags to lie on; others had nothing but the bare floor for a couch. There seemed to be no established rules among them; they were coming in at all hours, often through the night, in large numbers, and the Superintendent had enough to occupy his time in taking the names of those who came in, and of those who were sent out. His office was thronged through the day by persons who came to hire these poor creatures, who they say will not work and take care of themselves. Single women hire at four dollars a month; a woman with one child, two and a half or three dollars a month. Men's wages are ten dollars per month. Many of them, accustomed as they have been to field labor, and to living almost entirely out of doors, suffer much from the confinement in this crowded building. The little children pine like prison birds for their native element. It is almost impossible to keep the building in a healthy condition. Each day brings its fresh additions of the hungry, naked and sick. In the early part of June, there were, some days, as many as ten deaths reported at this place in twenty-four hours. At this time, there was no matron in the house, and nothing at hand to administer to the comfort of the sick and dying. I felt that their sufferings must be unknown to the people. I did not meet kindly, sympathizing people, trying to soothe the last agonies of death. Those tearful eyes often looked up to me with the language. "Is this freedom?"

A new Superintendent was engaged, Mr. Nichol, who seemed to understand what these people most needed. He laid down rules, went to work in earnest pulling down partitions to enlarge the rooms, that he might establish two hospitals, one for the men and another for the women. This accomplished, cots and matresses were needed. There is a small society in Washington—the Freedman's Association—who are doing all they can; but remember, Washington is not New England. I often met Rev. W.H. Channing, whose hands and heart are earnestly in the cause of the enslaved of his country. This gentleman was always ready to act in their behalf. Through these friends, an order was obtained from Gen. Wadsworth for cots for the contraband hospitals.

At this time, I met in Duff Green Row, Miss Hannah Stevenson, of Boston, and Miss Kendall. The names of these ladies need no comment. They were the first white females whom I had seen among these poor creatures, except those who had come in to hire them. These noble ladies had come to work, and their names will be lisped in prayer by many a dying slave. Hoping to help a little in the good work they had begun, I wrote to a lady in New York, a true and tried friend of the slave, who from the first moment had responded to every call of humanity. This letter was to ask for such articles as would make comfortable the sick and dying in the hospital. On the Saturday following, the cots were put up. A few hours after, an immense box was received from New York. Before the sun went down, those ladies who have labored so hard for the comfort of those people had the satisfaction of seeing every man, woman and child with clean garments, lying in a clean bed. What a contrast! They seemed different beings. Every countenance beamed with gratitude and satisfied rest. To me, it was a picture of holy peace within. The next day was the first Christian Sabbath they had ever known. One mother passed away as the setting sun threw its last rays across her dying bed, and as I looked upon her, I could not but say—"One day of freedom, and gone to her God." Before the dawn, others were laid beside her. It was a comfort to know that some effort had been made to soothe their dying pillows. Still, there were other places in which I felt, if possible, more interest, where the poor creatures seemed so far removed from the immediate sympathy of those who would help them. These were the contrabands in Alexandria. This place is strongly secesh; the inhabitants are kept quiet only at the point of Northern bayonets. In this place, the contrabands are distributed more over the city. In visiting those places, I had the assistance of two kind friends, women. True at heart, they felt the wrongs and degradation of their race. These ladies were always ready to aid me, as far as lay in their power. To Mrs. Brown, of 3d street, Washington, and Mrs. Dagans, of Alexandria, the contrabands owe much gratitude for the kindly aid they gave me in serving them. In this place, the men live in an old foundry, which does not afford protection from the weather. The sick lay on boards on the ground floor; some, through the kindness of the soldiers, have an old blanket. I did not hear a complaint among them. They said it was much better than it had been. All expressed a willingness to work, and were anxious to know what was to be done with them after the work was done. All of them said they had not received pay for their work, and some wanted to know if I thought it would be paid to their masters. One old man said, "I don't kere if dey don't pay, so dey give me freedom. I bin working for ole mass all de time; he nebber gib me five cent. I like de Unions fuss rate. If de Yankee Unions didn't come long, I'd be working tu de ole place now." All said they had plenty to eat, but no clothing, and no money to buy any.

Camps for Contrabands

Another place, the old school-house in Alexandria, is the Government head-quarters for the women. This I thought the most wretched of all the places. Any one who can find an apology for slavery should visit this place, and learn its curse. Here you see them from infancy up to a hundred years old. What but the love of freedom could bring these old people hither! One old man, who told me he was a hundred, said he had come to be free with his children. The journey proved too much for him. Each visit, I found him sitting in the same spot, under a shady tree, suffering from rheumatism. Unpacking a barrel, I found a large coat, which

I thought would be so nice for the old man, that I carried it to him. I found him sitting in the same spot, with his head on his bosom. I stooped down to speak to him. Raising his head, I found him dying. I called his wife. The old woman, who seems in her second childhood, looked on as quietly as though we were placing him for a night's rest. In this house are scores of women and children, with nothing to do, and nothing to do with. Their husbands are at work for the Government. Here they have food and shelter, but they cannot get work. The slaves who come into Washington from Maryland are sent here to protect them from the Fugitive Slave Law. These people are indebted to Mr. Rufus Leighton, formerly of Boston, for many comforts. But for their Northern friends, God pity them in their wretched and destitute condition! The Superintendent, Mr. Clarke, a Pennsylvanian, seems to feel much interest in them, and is certainly very kind. They told me they had confidence in him as a friend. That is much for a slave to say.

From this place, I went to Birch's slave-pen, in Alexandria. This place forms a singular contrast with what it was two years ago. The habitable part of the building is filled with contrabands; the old jail is filled with secesh prisoners—all within speaking distance of each other. Many a compliment is passed between them on the change in their positions. There is another house on Cameron street, which is filled with very destitute people. To these places I distributed large supplies of clothing, given me by the ladies of New York, New Bedford, and Boston. They have made many a desolate heart glad. They have clothed the naked, fed the hungry. To them, God's promise is sufficient.

Let me tell you of another place, to which I always planned my last visit for the day. There was something about this house to make you forget that you came to it with a heavy heart. The little children you meet at this door bring up pleasant memories when you leave it; from the older ones you carry pleasant recollections. These were what the people call the more favored slaves, and would boast of having lived in the first families in Virginia. They certainly had reaped some advantage from the contact. It seemed by a miracle that they had all fallen together. They were intelligent, and some of the young women and children beautiful. One young girl, whose beauty I cannot describe, although its magnetism often drew me to her side, I loved to talk with, and look upon her sweet face, covered with blushes; besides, I wanted to learn her true position, but her gentle shyness I had to respect. One day, while trying to draw her out, a fine-looking woman, with all the pride of a mother, stepped forward, and said—"Madam, this young woman is my son's wife." It was a relief. I thanked God that this young creature had an arm to lean upon for protection. Here I looked upon slavery, and felt the curse of their heritage was what is considered the best blood of Virginia. On one of my visits here, I met a mother who had just arrived from Virginia, bringing with her four daughters. Of course, they belonged to one of the first families. This man's strong attachment to this woman and her children caused her, with her children, to be locked up one month. She made her escape one day while her master had gone to learn the news from the Union army. She fled to the Northern army for freedom and protection. These people had earned for themselves many little comforts. Their houses had an inviting aspect. The clean floors, the clean white spreads on their cots, and the general tidiness throughout the building, convinced me they had done as well as any other race could have done, under the same circumstances.

Let me tell you of another place—Arlington Heights. Every lady has heard of [Confederate] Gen. [Robert E.] Lee's beautiful residence, which has been so faithfully guarded by our Northern army. It looks as though the master had given his orders every morning. Not a tree around that house has fallen. About the forts and camps they have been compelled to use the axe. At the quarters, there are many contrabands. The men are employed, and most of the women. Here they have plenty of exercise in the open air, and seem very happy. Many of the regiments are stationed here. It is a delightful place for both the soldier and the contraband. Looking around this place, and remembering what

I had heard of the character of the man who owned it before it passed into the hands of its present owner, I was much inclined to say, Although the wicked prosper for a season, the way of the transgressor is hard.

When in Washington for the day, my morning visit would be up at Duff Green's Row. My first business would be to look into a small room on the ground floor. This room was covered with lime. Here I would learn how many deaths had occurred in the last twenty-four hours. Men, women and children lie here together, without a shadow of those rites which we give to our poorest dead. There they lie, in the filthy rags they wore from the plantation. Nobody seems to give it a thought. It is an every-day occurrence, and the scenes have become familiar. One morning, as I looked in, I saw lying there five children. By the side of them lay a young man. He escaped, was taken back to Virginia, whipped nearly to death, escaped again the next night, dragged his body to Washington, and died, literally cut to pieces. Around his feet I saw a rope; I could not see that put into the grave with him. Other cases similar to this came to my knowledge, but this I saw.

Amid all this sadness, we sometimes would hear a shout of joy. Some mother had come in, and found her long-lost child; some husband his wife. Brothers and sisters meet. Some, without knowing it, had lived years within twenty miles of each other.

A word about the schools. It is pleasant to see that eager group of old and young, striving to learn their A, B, C, and Scripture sentences. Their great desire is to learn to read. While in the school-room, I could not but feel how much these young women and children needed female teachers who could do something more than teach them their A, B, C. They need to be taught the right habits of living and the true principles of life.

A Call for Help

My last visit intended for Alexandria was on Saturday. I spent the day with them, and received showers of thanks for myself and the good ladies who had sent me; for I had been careful to impress upon them that these kind friends sent me, and that all that was given by me was from them. Just as I was on the point of leaving, I found a young woman, with an infant, who had just been brought in. She lay in a dying condition, with nothing but a piece of an old soldier coat under her head. Must I leave her in this condition? I could not beg in Alexandria. It was time for the last boat to leave for Washington, and I promised to return in the morning. The Superintendent said he would meet me at the landing. Early next morning, Mrs. Brown and myself went on a begging expedition, and some old quilts were given us. Mr. Clarke met us, and offered the use of his large Government wagon, with the horses and driver, for the day, and said he would accompany us, if agreeable. I was delighted, and felt I should spend a happy Sabbath in exploring Dixie, while the large bundles that I carried with me would help make others happy. After attending to the sick mother and child, we started for Fairfax Seminary. They send many of the convalescent soldiers to this place. The houses are large, and the location is healthy. Many of the contrabands are here. Their condition is much better than that of those kept in the city. They soon gathered around Mr. Clarke, and begged him to come back and be their boss. He said, "Boys, I want you all to go to Hayti." They said, "You gwine wid us, Mr. Clarke!" "No, I must stay here, and take care of the rest of the boys." "Den, if you aint gwine, de Lord knows I aint a gwine." Some of them will tell Uncle Abe [Lincoln] the same thing. Mr. Clarke said they would do anything for him—seldom gave him any trouble. They spoke kindly of Mr. Thomas, who is constantly employed in supplying their wants, as far as he can. To the very old people at this place, I gave some clothing, returned to Alexandria, and bade all good bye. Begging me to come back they promised to do all they could to help themselves. One old woman said— "Honey tink, when all get still, I kin go an fine de old place? Tink de Union 'stroy it? You can't get nothin on dis place. Down on de ole place, you can raise ebery ting. I ain't seen bacca since I bin here. Neber git a libin here, where de peoples eben buy pasly." This poor old woman thought it was nice to live where tobacco grew, but it was dreadful to be compelled to buy a bunch of parsley. Here they have preaching once every Sabbath. They must have a season to sing and pray, and we need true faith in Christ to go among them and do our duty. How beautiful it is to find it among themselves! Do not say the slaves take no interest in each other. Like other people, some of them are designedly selfish, some are ignorantly selfish. With the light and instruction you give them, you will see this selfishness disappear. Trust them, make them free, and give them the responsibility of caring for themselves, and they will soon learn to help each other. Some of them have been so degraded by slavery that they do not know the usages of civilized life: they know little else than the overseer's lash. Have patience with them. You have helped to make them what they are: teach them civilization. You owe it to them, and you will find them as apt to learn as any other people that come to you stupid from oppression. The negroes' strong attachment no one doubts; the only difficulty is, they have cherished it too strongly. Let me tell you of an instance among the contrabands. One day, while in the hospital, a woman came in to ask that she might take a little orphan child. The mother had just died, leaving two children, the eldest three years old. This woman had five children in the house with her. In a few days, the number would be six. I said to this mother, "What can you do with this child, shut up here with your own? They are as many as you can attend to." She looked up with tears in her eyes, and said—"The child's mother was a stranger; none of her friends cum wid her from de ole place. I took one boy down on de plantation; he is a big boy now, working mong de Unions. De Lord help me to bring up dat boy, and he will help me to take care dis child. My husband work for de Unions when dey pay him. I can make home for all. Dis child shall hab part ob de crust." How few white mothers, living in luxury, with six children, could find room in her heart for a seventh, and that child a stranger!

In this house there are scores of children, too young to help themselves, from eight years old down to the little one-day freeman, born at railroad speed, while the young mother was flying from Virginia to save her babe from breathing its tainted air.

I left the contrabands, feeling that the people were becoming more interested in their behalf, and much had been done to make their condition more comfortable. On my way home, I stopped a few days in Philadelphia. I called on a lady who had sent a large supply to the hospital, and told her of the many little orphans who needed a home. This lady advised me to call and see the Lady Managers of an institution for orphan children supported by those ladies. I did so, and they agreed to take the little orphans. They employed a gentleman to investigate the matter, and it was found impossible to bring them through Baltimore. This gentleman went to the captains of the propellers in Philadelphia, and asked if those orphan children could have a passage on their boats. Oh no, it could not be; it would make an unpleasant feeling among the people! Some of those orphans have died since I left, but the number is constantly increasing. Many mothers, on leaving the plantations, pick up the little orphans, and bring them with their own children; but they cannot provide for them; they come very destitute themselves.

To the ladies who have so nobly interested themselves in behalf of my much oppressed race, I feel the deepest debt of gratitude. Let me beg the reader's attention to these orphans. They are the innocent and helpless of God's poor. If you cannot take one, you can do much by contributing your mite to the institution that will open its doors to receive them.

A Day of Celebration for Abolitionists

Charlotte Forten Grimké

January 1, 1863, the date that President Abraham Lincoln issued the Emancipation Proclamation, was a day of joyous victory celebrations for all abolitionists. On that day, Charlotte Forten, born in 1837 into a wealthy, educated black family in Philadelphia, was serving as a volunteer on the island of Port Royal off the coast of South Carolina. The Union troops who controlled the island had set up a camp where refugee slaves could be safely lodged and offered work and literacy training. As part of the so-called Port Royal Experiment, Colonel Thomas Wentworth Higginson, a white Boston abolitionist, had begun training young African American men for service in the Union army. Forten recorded in her journal the events of January 1, 1863, highlighting ceremonies marking the Emancipation Proclamation and a dress parade of African American soldiers. After the war, Forten married Francis Grimké, who would graduate from the Princeton Theological Seminary and become a leading African American clergyman of the late-nineteenth century. The Forten journal remained unpublished until 1953.

Thursday, New Year's Day, 1863. The most glorious day this nation has yet seen, I think. I rose early—an event here—and early we started, with an old borrowed carriage and a remarkably slow horse. Whither were we going? thou wilt ask, dearest A. To the ferry; thence to Camp Saxton, to

Charlotte Forten Grimké, *The Journals of Charlotte Forten Grimké*, New York: Oxford University Press, 1988.

the Celebration. From the Ferry to the camp the "Flora" took us.

How pleasant it was on board! A crowd of people, whites and blacks, and a band of music—to the great delight of the negroes. Met on board Dr. and Mrs. Peck and their daughters, who greeted me most kindly. Also Gen. S[axton]'s father whom I like much, and several other acquaintances whom I was glad to see. We stopped at Beaufort, and then proceeded to Camp Saxton, the camp of the 1st Reg[iment] S[outh] C[arolina] Vol[unteer]s. The "Flora" c[ou]ld not get up to the landing, so we were rowed ashore in a row boat.

Just as my foot touched the plank, on landing, a hand grasped mine and well known voice spoke my name. It was my dear and noble friend, Dr. Rogers. I cannot tell you, dear A., how delighted I was to see him; how *good* it was to see the face of a friend from the North, and *such* a friend. I think myself particularly blessed to have him for a friend. Walking on a little distance I found myself being presented to Col. Higginson, whereat I was so much overwhelmed, that I had no reply to make to the very kind and courteous little speech with which he met me. I believe I mumbled something, and grinned like a simpleton, that was all. Provoking, isn't it? that when one is most in need of sensible words, one finds them not.

Celebrating Emancipation

I *cannot* give a regular chronicle of the day. It is impossible. I was in such a state of excitement. It all seemed, and seems still, like a brilliant dream. Dr. R[ogers] and I talked all the time, I know, while he showed me the camp and all the arrangements. They have a beautiful situation, on the grounds once occupied by a very old fort, "De La Ribanchine," built in 1629 or 30. Some of the walls are still standing. Dr. R[ogers] has made quite a good hospital out of an old gin house. I went over it. There are only a few invalids in it, at present. I saw everything; the kitchens, cooking arrangements, and all. Then we took seats on the platform.

The meeting was held in a beautiful grove, a live-oak

grove, adjoining the camp. It is the largest one I have yet seen; but I don't think the moss pendants are quite as beautiful as they are on St. Helena. As I sat on the stand and looked around on the various groups, I thought I had never seen a sight so beautiful. There were the black soldiers, in their blue coats and scarlet pants, the officers of this and other regiments in their handsome uniforms, and crowds of lookers-on, men, women and children, grouped in various attitudes, under the trees. The faces of all wore a happy, eager, expectant look.

The exercises commenced by a prayer from Rev. Mr. Fowler, Chaplain of the reg[iment]. An ode written for the occasion by Prof. Zachos, originally a Greek, now Sup[erintendent] of Paris island—was read by himself, and then sung by the whites. Col. H[igginson] introduced Dr. Brisbane in a few elegant and graceful words. He (Dr. B.) read the President's [Emancipation] Proclamation, which was warmly cheered. Then the beautiful flags presented by Dr. Cheever's Church [in New York] were presented to Col. H[igginson] for the Reg[iment] in an excellent and enthusiastic speech, by Rev. Mr. [Mansfield] French. Immediately at the conclu-

Lincoln issued the Emancipation Proclamation in 1863, which freed slaves in states rebelling against the Union and helped to end the Civil War.

sion, some of the colored people—of their own accord sang "My Country Tis of Thee." It was a touching and beautiful incident, and Col. Higginson, in accepting the flags made it the occasion of some happy remarks. He said that *that* tribute was far more effective than any speech he c'ld make. He spoke for some time, and all that he said was grand, glorious. He seemed inspired. Nothing c'ld have been better, more perfect. And Dr. R[ogers] told me afterward that the Col. was much affected. That tears were in his eyes. He is as Whittier says, truly a "sure man." The men all admire and love him. There is a great deal of personal magnetism about him, and his kindness is proverbial. After he had done speaking he delivered the flags to the color-bearers with a few very impressive remarks to them. They each then, Sgt. Prince Rivers and [Cpl.] Robert Sutton made very good speeches indeed, and were loudly cheered. Gen. Saxton and Mrs. Gage spoke very well. The good Gen. was received with great enthusiasm, and throughout the morning—every little while it seemed to me three cheers were given for him. A Hymn written I believe, by Mr. Judd, was sung, and then all the people united with the Reg[iment] in singing "John Brown." It was grand. During the exercises, it was announced that Fremont was appointed Commander-in chief of the Army, and this was received with enthusiastic and prolonged cheering. But as it is picket news, I greatly fear that is not true.

A Visit with Colonel Higginson

We dined with good Dr. R[ogers] at the Col's [T. W. Higginson] table, though, greatly to my regret he, (the Col.) was not there. He partook of some of the oxen, (of which ten had been roasted) with his men. I like his doing that. We had quite a sumptuous dinner. Our party consisted of Dr. R[ogers], Adjutant D[ewhurst], Capt. R[ogers], Mr. and Miss Ware (Mrs. Winsor's brother and sister), Mr. Hall, their cousin, whom I like much, and Mr. and Miss H[unn] and me. We had a merry, delightful dinner. The only part that I did not enjoy was being obliged to read Whittier's Hymn aloud at the table. I wanted Dr. R[ogers] to do it. But he w'ld insist on my doing it. So of course it was murdered. I believe the older I grow the more averse I get to doing anything in public. I have no courage to do such things.

Col. H[igginson] invited us into his tent—a very nice, almost *homelike* one. I noticed a nice secretary, with writing utensils and "Les Miserables" on it. A *wreath* of beautiful oranges hung against the wall, fronting the door. I wanted to have a good look at this tent; but we were hardly seated when the Dr. and Col. were called away for a moment, and Lieut. Col. Billings coming in w'ld insist upon our going into his tent. I did not want to go at all, but he was so *persistent* we had to. I fear he is a somewhat vain person. His tent was very comfortable too, and I noticed quite a large piece of "Secesh" furniture, something between a secretary and a bureau, and quite a collection of photographs and daguerres. But I did not examine them, for my attention was occupied by Col. H[igginson] to whom I showed Whittier's poem, letter and photo. "He looks old," he said to me sadly, as he handed back the picture.

Dr. R[ogers] introduced me to Dr. H[awks] and his wife—pleasant people, and *good* anti-slavery. They mentioned having Liberators with my letters in them. I am sorry they have come down here.

Col. H[igginson] asked me to go out and hear the band play, which I very gladly did. But it stopped just as we stepped outside of the tent. Just then one of the soldiers came up to the Col. and said "Do Cunnel, do ask 'em to play Dixie, just for me, for my lone self." The Col. made the request, but the leader of the band said he feared they w'ld not be able to play the whole tune as they had not the necessary pieces. "Nebber mind," said the man "jus' half a tune will do." It was found impossible to play even that but the leader promised that the next time they came they would be fully prepared to play Dixie for him.

A Dress Parade

The Dress Parade—the first I had ever seen—delighted me. It was a brilliant sight—the long line of men in their bril-

liant uniform, with bayonets gleaming in the sunlight. The
Col. looked splendid. The Dr. said the men went through
with the drill remarkably well. It seemed to me nothing c'ld
be more perfect. To me it was a grand triumph—that black
regiment doing itself honor in the sight of the white officers,
many of whom, doubtless "came to scoff." It was typical of
what the race, so long down-trodden and degraded will yet
achieve on this Continent.

After the Parade, we went to the Landing, intending to
take a boat for Beaufort. But the boat was too crowded, and
we decided to wait for another. It was the softest, loveliest
moonlight. We sat down among the ruins of the old fort. Just
[as soon] as the boat had reached a favorable distance from
the shore the band in it commenced playing Home, sweet
Home. It was exquisitely beautiful. The lovely moonlight on
the water, the perfect stillness around seemed to give new
beauty to that ever beautiful old song. And then as my dear
friend, Dr. R[ogers] said, "It came *very near* to us all."

Finding the night air damp we went to the tent of Mr.
Fowler, the chaplain, whom I like much better in private
conversation than as an orator. He is a thoroughly good,
earnest man. Thither came Col. H[igginson] and Dr.
H[awks]. We sat around the nice fire—the tent has *chimney*
and fire place, made by Mr. F[owler]'s own skilful hands.
Col. H[igginson] is a perfectly delightful person in private.—So genial, so witty, so kind. But I noticed when he
was silent, a careworn almost sad expression on his earnest,
noble face. My heart was full when I looked at him. I longed
to say "I thank you, I thank you, for that noble glorious
speech." And yet I *c'ld not*. It is always so. I do not know
how to talk. Words always fail me when I want them most.
The more I feel the more impossible it is for me to speak. It
is very provoking. Among other things, Col. H[igginson]
said how amusing it was to him—their plan of housekeeping down here. "This morning I was asked "Well, Colonel,
how many oxen shall we roast today." And I said, just as
calmly as I w'ld have ordered a pound or two of beef, at
home.—well I think *ten* will do. And then to be consulted

as to how many gallons of molasses, and of vinegar, and how many pounds of ginger w'ld be wanted seemed very odd." I wish I c'ld reproduce for you the dry humorous tones in which this was said. We had a pleasant chat, sitting there in the firelight, and I was most unwilling to go, for besides the happiness of being in the society of the Col. and the Dr. we wanted dreadfully to see the "shout" and grand jubilee which the soldiers were going to have that night. But it was already late, and hearing that the "Flora" was coming we had to hasten to the Landing. I was sorry to say good-bye to Dr. R[ogers]. What an *unspeakable* happiness it was to see him. But I fear for his health. I fear the exposure of a camp life. Am glad to see that he has warm robes and blankets, to keep him comfortable. I wish I c'ld do something for him. He has done so much for me.

The Dawn of Freedom

Ah, what a grand, glorious day this has been. The dawn of freedom which it heralds may not break upon us at once; but it will surely come, and sooner, I believe, than we have ever dared hope before. My soul is glad with an exceeding great gladness. But before I close, dear A., I must bring our little party safe home to Oaklands. We had a good time on the Flora. L[izzie Hunn] and I promenaded the deck, and sang John Brown, and Whittier's Hymn and "My Country Tis of Thee." And the moon shone bright above us, and the waves beneath, smooth and clear, glistened in the soft moonlight. At Beaufort we took the row boat, and the boatmen sang as they rowed us across. Mr. Hall was with us, and seemed really to appreciate and enjoy everything. I like him. Arrived at St. Helena's we separated, he to go to "Coffin's Point" (a dreadful name, as Dr. R[ogers] says) and we to come hither [Oaklands]. Can't say that I enjoyed the homeward drive very much. T'was so intensely cold, yes *intensely*, for these regions. I fear some of the hot enthusiasm with which my soul was filled got chilled a little but it was only for a short time.

Old friend, my good and dear A. a very, very happy New Year to you! Dear friends in both my Northern homes a happy, happy New Year to you, too! And to us all a year of such freedom as we have never yet known in this boasted but hitherto wicked land. The hymn, or rather one of the hymns that those boat[men] sung [*sic*] is singing itself to me now. The refrain "Religion so . . . sweet" was so sweet and touching in its solemnity.

Reconstruction and the Needs of the American Negro

Frederick Douglass

> After emancipation, Frederick Douglass, the leading black
> abolitionist, turned his attention to the plight of the former
> slaves in American society. He agitated for voting rights, edu-
> cational opportunities, and social and economic equality for
> all African Americans. In this article on Reconstruction,
> which originally appeared in the December 1866 issue of *The
> Atlantic Monthly*, Douglass outlines the issues concerning the
> place of blacks in postwar society—issues to which he, other
> black reformers, and white civil rights activists would devote
> themselves during the decades following the Civil War.

The assembling of the Second Session of the Thirty-ninth
Congress may very properly be made the occasion of a
few earnest words on the already much-worn topic of reconstruction.

Seldom has any legislative body been the subject of a so-
licitude more intense, or of aspirations more sincere and ardent. There are the best of reasons for this profound interest. Questions of vast moment, left undecided by the last
session of Congress, must be manfully grappled with by
this. No political skirmishing will avail. The occasion demands statesmanship.

Whether the tremendous war so heroically fought and so

Frederick Douglass, *Selected Speeches and Writings*, edited by Philip S. Foner, Chicago:
Lawrence Hill Books, 1999.

victoriously ended shall pass into history a miserable failure, barren of permanent results,—a scandalous and shock-
ing waste of blood and treasure,—a strife for empire, as Earl
Russell characterized it, of no value to liberty or civilization,—an attempt to reestablish a Union by force, which
must be the merest mockery of a Union,—an effort to bring
under Federal authority States into which no loyal man from
the North may safely enter, and to bring men into the national councils who deliberate with daggers and vote with
revolvers, and who do not even conceal their deadly hate of
the country that conquered them; or whether, on the other
hand, we shall, as the rightful reward of victory over trea-
son, have a solid nation, entirely delivered from all contra-
dictions and social antagonisms, based upon loyalty, liberty,
and equality, must be determined one way or the other by
the present session of Congress. The last session really did
nothing which can be considered final as to these questions.
The Civil Rights Bill and the Freedmen's Bureau Bill and
the proposed constitutional amendments, with the amendment already adopted and recognized as the law of the land,
do not reach the difficulty, and cannot, unless the whole
structure of the government is changed from a government
by States to something like a despotic central government,
with power to control even the municipal regulations of
States, and to make them conform to its own despotic will.
While there remains such an idea as the right of each State
to control its own local affairs,—an idea, by the way, more
deeply rooted in the minds of men of all sections of the
country than perhaps any one other political idea,—no general assertion of human rights can be of any practical value.
To change the character of the government at this point is
neither possible nor desirable. All that is necessary to be
done is to make the government consistent with itself, and
render the rights of the States compatible with the sacred
rights of human nature.

The arm of the Federal government is long, but it is far
too short to protect the rights of individuals in the interior
of distant States. They must have the power to protect them-

selves, or they will go unprotected, spite of all the laws the Federal government can put upon the national Statute-book.

Slavery, like all other great systems of wrong, founded in the depths of human selfishness, and existing for ages, has not neglected its own conservation. It has steadily exerted an influence upon all around it favorable to its own continuance. And to-day it is so strong that it could exist, not only without law, but even against law. Custom, manners, morals, religion, are all on its side everywhere in the South; and when you add the ignorance and servility of the ex-slave to the intelligence and accustomed authority of the master, you have the conditions, not out of which slavery will again grow, but under which it is impossible for the Federal government to wholly destroy it, unless the Federal government be armed with despotic power, to blot out State authority, and to station a Federal officer at every cross-road. This, of course, cannot be done, and ought not even if it could. The true way and the easiest way is to make our government entirely consistent with itself, and give to every loyal citizen the elective franchise,—a right and power which will be ever present, and will form a wall of fire for his protection.

Protecting Citizens' Rights

One of the invaluable compensations of the late Rebellion is the highly instructive disclosure it made of the true source of danger to republican government. Whatever may be tolerated in monarchical and despotic governments, no republic is safe that tolerates a privileged class, or denies to any of its citizens equal rights and equal means to maintain them. What was theory before the war has been made fact by the war.

There is cause to be thankful even for rebellion. It is an impressive teacher, though a stern and terrible one. In both characters it has come to us, and it was perhaps needed in both. It is an instructor never a day before its time, for it comes only when all other means of progress and enlightenment have failed. Whether the oppressed and despairing bondman, no longer able to repress his deep yearnings for manhood, or the tyrant, in his pride and impatience, takes initiative, and strikes the blow for a firmer hold and a longer lease of oppression, the result is the same,—society is instructed, or may be.

Such are the limitations of the common mind, and so thoroughly engrossing are the cares of common life, that only the few among men can discern through the glitter and dazzle of present prosperity the dark outlines of approaching disasters, even though they may have come up to our very gates, and are already within striking distance. The yawning seam and corroded bolt conceal their defects from the mariner until the storm calls all hands to the pumps. Prophets indeed, were abundant before the war; but who cares for prophets while their predictions remain unfulfilled, and the calamities of which they tell are masked behind a blinding blaze of national prosperity?

The War Uprooted Slavery

It is asked, said Henry Clay, on a memorable occasion, Will slavery never come to an end? That question, said he, was asked fifty years ago, and it has been answered by fifty years of unprecedented prosperity. Spite of the eloquence of the earnest Abolitionists,—poured out against slavery during thirty years,—even they must confess, that, in all the probabilities of the case, that system of barbarism would have continued its horrors far beyond the limits of the nineteenth century but for the Rebellion, and perhaps only have disappeared at last in a fiery conflict, even more fierce and bloody than that which has now been suppressed.

It is no disparagement to truth, that it can only prevail where reason prevails. War begins where reason ends. The thing worse than rebellion is the thing that causes rebellion. What that thing is, we have been taught to our cost. It remains now to be seen whether we have the needed courage to have that cause entirely removed from the Republic. At any rate, to this grand work of national regeneration and entire purification Congress must now address itself, with full purpose that the work shall this time be thoroughly done.

The deadly upas, root and branch, leaf and fibre, body and sap, must be utterly destroyed. The country is evidently not in a condition to listen patiently to pleas for postponement, however plausible, nor will it permit the responsibility to be shifted to other shoulders. Authority and power are here commensurate with the duty imposed. There are no cloud-flung shadows to obscure the way. Truth shines with brighter light and intenser heat at every moment, and a country torn and rent and bleeding implores relief from its distress and agony.

Congress Must Act

If time was at first needed, Congress has now had time. All the requisite materials from which to form an intelligent judgment are now before it. Whether its members look at the origin, the progress, the termination of the war, or at the mockery of a peace now existing, they will find only one un-broken chain of argument in favor of a radical policy of re-construction. For the omissions of the last session, some ex-cuses may be allowed. A treacherous President [Andrew Johnson] stood in the way; and it can be easily seen how re-luctant good men might be to admit an apostasy which in-volved so much of baseness and ingratitude. It was natural that they should seek to save him by bending to him even when he leaned to the side of error. But all is changed now. Congress knows now that it must go on without his aid, and even against his machinations. The advantage of the present session over the last is immense. Where that investigated, this has the facts. Where that walked by faith, this may walk by sight. Where that halted, this must go forward, and where that failed, this must succeed, giving the country whole mea-sures where that gave us half-measures, merely as a means of saving the elections in a few doubtful districts. That Con-gress saw what was right, but distrusted the enlightenment of the loyal masses; but what was forborne in distrust of the people must now be done with a full knowledge that the people expect and require it. The members go to Washing-ton fresh from the inspiring presence of the people. In every considerable public meeting, and in almost every conceivable way, whether at court-house, school-house, or crossroads, in doors and out, the subject has been discussed, and the people have emphatically pronounced in favor of a radical policy. Listening to the doctrines of expediency and compromise with pity, impatience, and disgust, they have everywhere broken into demonstrations of the wildest enthusiasm when a brave word has been spoken in favor of equal rights and impartial suffrage. Radicalism, so far from being odious, is now the popular passport to power. The men most bitterly charged with it go to Congress with the largest majorities, while the timid and doubtful are sent by lean majorities, or

Support for the Civil Rights Act of 1875

Early in 1874, the U.S. Congress began discussing civil rights legislation that would support the Fourteenth Amendment's guarantee for equal protection of the law for all American citizens. Robert Brown Elliot, a black congressman from South Carolina, offered his support for this legislation in a speech delivered on the floor of the House of Representatives.

The results of the war, as seen in reconstruction, have settled forever the political status of my race. The passage of this bill will determine the civil status, not only of the Negro, but of any other class of citizens who may feel themselves discriminated against. It will form the capstone of that temple of liberty, begun on this continent under discouraging circumstances . . . until at last it stands in all its beautiful symmetry and proportions, a building the grandest which the world has ever seen, realizing the most sanguine expectations and the highest hopes of those who, in the name of equal, impartial, and universal liberty, laid the foundation stones.

Sanford Wexler, *The Civil Rights Movement: An Eyewitness History.* New York: Facts On File, 1993, p. 20.

else left at home. The strange controversy between the President and Congress, at one time so threatening, is disposed of by the people. The high reconstructive powers which he so confidently, ostentatiously, and haughtily claimed, have been disallowed, denounced, and utterly repudiated; while those claimed by Congress have been confirmed.

Of the spirit and magnitude of the canvass nothing need be said. The appeal was to the people, and the verdict was worthy of the tribunal. Upon an occasion of his own selection, with the advice and approval of his astute Secretary, soon after the members of Congress had returned to their constituents, the President quitted the executive mansion, sandwiched himself between two recognized heroes,—men whom the whole country delighted to honor,—and, with all the advantage which such company could give him, stumped the country from the Atlantic to the Mississippi, advocating everywhere his policy as against that of Congress. It was a strange sight, and perhaps the most disgraceful exhibition ever made by any President; but, as no evil is entirely unmixed, good has come of this, as from many others. Ambitious, unscrupulous, energetic, indefatigable, voluble, and plausible,—a political gladiator, ready for a "set-to" in any crowd,—he is beaten in his own chosen field, and stands to-day before the country as a convicted usurper, a political criminal, guilty of a bold and persistent attempt to possess himself of the legislative powers solemnly secured to Congress by the Constitution. No vindication could be more complete, no condemnation could be more absolute and humiliating. Unless reopened by the sword, as recklessly threatened in some circles, this question is now closed for all time.

Without attempting to settle here the metaphysical and somewhat theological question (about which so much has already been said and written), whether once in the Union means always in the Union,—agreeably to the formula, once in grace always in grace,—it is obvious to common sense that the rebellious States stand to-day, in point of law, precisely where they stood when, exhausted, beaten, conquered, they fell powerless at the feet of Federal authority. Their State governments were overthrown, and the lives and property of the leaders of the Rebellion were forfeited. In reconstructing the institutions of these shattered and overthrown States, Congress should begin with a clean slate, and make clean work of it. Let there be no hesitation. It would be a cowardly deference to a defeated and treacherous President, if any account were made of the illegitimate, one-sided, sham governments hurried into existence for a malign purpose in the absence of Congress. These pretended governments, which were never submitted to the people, and from participation in which four millions of the loyal people were excluded by Presidential order, should now be treated according to their true character, as shams and impositions and supplanted by true and legitimate governments, in the formation of which loyal men, black and white, shall participate.

Reconstructing the Nation

It is not, however, within the scope of this paper to point out the precise steps to be taken, and the means to be employed. The people are less concerned about these than the grand end to be attained. They demand such a reconstruction as shall put an end to the present anarchical state of things in the late rebellious States,—where frightful murders and wholesale massacres are perpetrated in the very presence of Federal soldiers. This horrible business they require shall cease. They want a reconstruction such as will protect loyal men, black and white, in their persons and property; such a one as will cause Northern industry, Northern capital, and Northern civilization to flow into the South, and make a man from New England as much at home in Carolina as elsewhere in the Republic. No Chinese wall can now be tolerated. The South must be opened to the light of law and liberty, and this session of Congress is relied upon to accomplish this important work.

The plain, common-sense way of doing this work, as intimated at the beginning, is simply to establish in the South one law, one government, one administration of justice, one condition to the exercise of the elective franchise, for men of all races and colors alike. This great measure is sought as earnestly by loyal white men as by loyal blacks, and is needed alike by both. Let sound political prescience but take the place of an unreasoning prejudice, and this will be done.

Men denounce the Negro for his prominence in this discussion; but it is no fault of his that in peace as in war, that in conquering Rebel armies as in reconstructing the rebellious States, the right of the Negro is the true solution of our national troubles. The stern logic of events, which goes directly to the point, disdaining all concern for the color or features of men, has determined the interests of the country as identical with and inseparable from those of the Negro.

The policy that emancipated and armed the Negro—now seen to have been wise and proper by the dullest—was not certainly more sternly demanded than is now the policy of enfranchisement. If with the Negro was success in war, and without him failure, so in peace it will be found that the nation must fall or flourish with the Negro.

Fortunately, the Constitution of the United States knows no distinction between citizens on account of color. Neither does it know any difference between a citizen of a State and a citizen of the United States. Citizenship evidently includes all the rights of citizens, whether State or national. If the Constitution knows none, it is clearly no part of the duty of a Republican Congress now to institute one. The mistake of the last session was the attempt to do this very thing, by a renunciation of its power to secure political rights to any class of citizens, with the obvious purpose to allow the rebellious States to disfranchise, if they should see fit, their colored citizens. This unfortunate blunder must now be retrieved, and the emasculated citizenship given to the Negro supplanted by that contemplated in the Constitution of the United States, which declares that the citizens of each State shall enjoy all the rights and immunities of citizens of the several States,—so that a legal voter in any State shall be a legal voter in all the States.

The Role of Colored Women in Postwar American Society

Frances Watkins Harper

Frances Watkins Harper was born free in the slave state of
Maryland in 1825. As a young woman, she became deeply
involved in the abolitionist movement. She worked for the
Underground Railroad, delivered antislavery speeches
throughout the North, published abolitionist poetry, and contributed articles to abolitionist newspapers. She also wrote
fiction. Her most noteworthy fictional work was *Iola Leroy*, a
novel published in 1892. After the Civil War, Harper became
involved in a number of reform movements, including the
effort to secure equal political rights and economic opportunities for women. Harper delivered this speech on the role of
African American women in post–Civil War American society to the Women's Congress in 1877. It was later published
as "Coloured Women in America" in the January 1878 issue
of *Englishwoman's Review*.

The women as a class are quite equal to the men in energy and executive ability. In fact I find by close obser-
vation, that the mothers are the levers which move in education. The men talk about it, especially about election time,
if they want an office for self or their candidate, but the
women work most for it. They labour in many ways to support the family, while the children attend school. They make

Frances Watkins Harper, *A Brighter Coming Day: A Frances Ellen Watkins Harper
Reader*, edited by Frances Smith Foster, New York: Feminist Press, 1990.

great sacrifices to spare their own children during school hours. I know of girls from sixteen to twenty-two who iron till midnight that they may come to school in the day. Some of our scholars, aged about nineteen, living about thirty miles off, rented land, ploughed, planted, and then sold their cotton, in order to come to us. A woman near me, urged her husband to go in debt 500 dollars for a home, as the titles to the land they built on were insecure, and she said to me, "We have five years to pay it in, and I shall begin to-day to do it, if life is spared. I will make a hundred dollars at washing, for I have done it." Yet they have seven little children to feed, clothe, and educate. In the field the women receive the same wages as the men, and are often preferred, clearing land, hoeing, or picking cotton, with equal ability.

In different departments of business, coloured women have not only been enabled to keep the wolf from the door, but also to acquire property, and in some cases the coloured woman is the mainstay of the family, and when work fails the men in large cities, the money which the wife can obtain by washing, ironing, and other services, often keeps pauperism at bay. I do not suppose, considering the state of her industrial lore and her limited advantages, that there is among the poorer classes a more helpful woman than the coloured woman as a labourer. When I was in Mississippi, I stopped with Mr. Montgomery, a former slave of Jefferson Davis's brother. His wife was a woman capable of taking on her hands 130 acres of land, and raising one hundred and seven bales of cotton by the force which she could organise. Since then I have received a very interesting letter from her daughter, who for years has held the position of Assistant Post-mistress. In her letter she says: "There are many women around me who would serve as models of executiveness anywhere. They do double duty, a man's share in the field, and a woman's part at home. They do any kind of field work, even ploughing, and at home the cooking, washing, milking, and gardening. But these have husbands; let me tell you of some widows and unaided women:—

"1st. Mrs. Hill, a widow, has rented, cultivated, and solely managed a farm of five acres for five years. She makes her garden, raises poultry, and cultivates enough corn and cotton to live comfortably, and keep a surplus in the bank. She saves something every year, and this is much, considering the low price of cotton and unfavourable seasons.

"2nd. Another woman, whose husband died in the service during the war, cultivated one acre, making vegetables for sale, besides a little cotton. She raises poultry, spins thread, and knits hose for a living. She supports herself comfortably, never having to ask credit or to borrow.

"[3rd.] Mrs. Jane Brown and Mrs. Halsey formed a partnership about ten years ago, leased nine acres and a horse, and have cultivated the land all that time, just the same as men would have done. They have saved considerable money from year to year, and are living independently. They have never had any expenses for labour, making and gathering the crops themselves.

"4th. Mrs. Henry, by farming and peddling cakes, has the last seven years laid up seven hundred dollars. She is an invalid, and unable to work at all times. Since then she has been engaged in planting sweet potatoes and raising poultry and hogs. Last year she succeeded in raising 250 hogs, but lost two-thirds by disease. She furnished eggs and chickens enough for family use, and sold a surplus of chickens, say fifty dozen chickens. On nine acres she made 600 bushels of sweet potatoes. The present year she has planted ten acres of potatoes. She has 100 hogs, thirty dozen chickens, a small lot of ducks and turkeys, and also a few sheep and goats. She has also a large garden under her supervision, which is planted in cabbages. She has two women and a boy to assist. Miss Montgomery, a coloured lady, says: 'I have constantly been engaged in bookkeeping for eight years, and for ten years as assistant post-mistress, doing all the work of the office. Now, instead of bookkeeping, I manage a school of 133 pupils, and I have an assistant, and I am still attending to the post-office.' Of her sister she says, she is a better and swifter worker than herself; that she generally sews, but that last year she made 100 dozen jars of preserved fruit for sale. An acquaintance of mine, who lives in South Carolina, and has been engaged in mission work, reports that, in supporting the family, women are the mainstay; that two-thirds of the truck gardening is done by them in South Carolina; that in the city they are more industrious than the men; that when the men lose their work through their political affiliations, the women stand by them, and say, 'stand by your principles.' And I have been informed by the same person that a number of women have homes of their own, bought by their hard earnings since freedom. Mr. Stewart, who was employed in the Freedmen's bank, says he has seen scores of coloured women in the South working and managing plantations of from twenty to 100 acres. They and their boys and girls doing all the labour, and marketing in the fall from ten to fifty bales of cotton. He speaks of a mulatto woman who rented land, which she and her children worked until they had made enough to purchase a farm of 130 acres. She then lived alone upon it, hiring help and working it herself, making a comfortable living, and assisting her sons in the purchase of land. The best sugar maker, he observes, he ever saw was a stupid looking coloured woman, apparently twenty-five years old. With a score or more of labourers, she was the 'boss,' and it was her eye which detected the exact consistency to which the syrup had boiled, and, while tossing it in the air, she told with certainty the point of granulation."

Women in High Places

In higher walks of life too, the coloured women have made progress. The principal of the Coloured High School in Philadelphia was born a slave in the District of Columbia; but in early life she was taken North, and she resolved to get knowledge. When about fifteen years old, she obtained a situation as a house servant, with the privilege of going every other day to receive instruction. Poverty was in her way, but instead of making it a stumbling block, she converted it into a stepping stone. She lived in one place about six years, and received seven dollars a month. A coloured lady presented her a scholarship, and she entered Oberlin as a pupil. When she was sufficiently advanced, Oberlin was brave enough to accord her a place as a teacher in the preparatory department of the college, a position she has held for several years, graduating almost every year a number of pupils, a part of whom are scattered abroad as teachers in different parts of the country. Nearly all the coloured teachers in Washington are girls and women, a large percentage of whom were educated in the district of Columbia. Nor is it only in the ranks of teachers that coloured women are content to remain. Some years since, two coloured women were studying in the Law School of Howard University. One of them, Miss Charlotte Ray, a member of this body, has since graduated, being, I believe, the first coloured woman in the country who has ever gained the distinction of being a graduated lawyer. Others have gone into medicine and have been practising in different States of the Union. In the Woman's Medical College of Pennsylvania, two coloured women were last year pursuing their studies as Matriculants, while a young woman, the daughter of a former fugitive slave, has held the position of an assistant resident physician in one of the hospitals. Miss Cole, of Philadelphia, held for some time the position of physician in the State Orphan Asylum in South Carolina.

In literature and art we have not accomplished much, although we have a few among us who have tried literature. Miss Foster has written for the *Atlantic Monthly*, and Mrs. Mary Shadd Cary for years edited a paper called the *Provincial Freeman*, and another coloured woman has written several stories, poems, and sketches, which have appeared in different periodicals. In art, we have Miss Edmonia Lewis, who is, I believe, allied on one side to the negro race. She exhibited several pieces of statuary, among which is Cleopatra, at the Centennial.

Working for Charities

The coloured women have not been backward in promoting charities for their own sex and race. One of the most efficient helpers is Mrs. Madison, who although living in a humble and unpretending home, had succeeded in getting up a home for aged coloured women. By organized effort, coloured women have been enabled to help each other in sickness, and provide respectable funerals for the dead. They have institutions under different names; one of the oldest, perhaps the oldest in the country, has been in existence, as I have been informed, about fifty years, and has been officered and managed almost solely by women for about half a century. There are also, in several States, homes for aged coloured women: the largest I know of being in Philadelphia. This home was in a measure built by Stephen and Harriet Smith, coloured citizens of the State of Pennsylvania. Into this home men are also admitted. The city of Philadelphia has also another home for the homeless, which, besides giving them a temporary shelter, provides a permanent home for a number of aged coloured women. In looking over the statistics of miscellaneous charities, out of a list of fifty-seven charitable institutions, I see only nine in which there is any record of coloured inmates. Out of twenty-six Industrial Schools, I counted four. Out of a list of one hundred and fifty-seven orphan asylums, miscellaneous charities, and industrial schools, I find fifteen asylums in which there is some mention of coloured inmates. More than half the reform schools in 1874, had admitted coloured girls. The coloured women of Philadelphia have formed a Christian Relief Association, which has opened sewing schools for coloured girls, and which has been enabled, year after year, to lend a hand to some of the more needy of their race, and it also has, I understand, sustained an employment office for some time.

Chapter 3

Booker T. Washington and His Critics

Chapter Preface

At the turn of the nineteenth century, Booker T. Washington emerged as the successor to Frederick Douglass as the leading African American reformer. His personal story was compelling. He was born a slave in Virginia in 1856; through hard work and determination, he obtained an education at Hampton Institute, a school in Hampton, Virginia, established for black and Native American students after the Civil War. In 1881 he was named director of the Tuskegee Institute, an industrial college in rural Alabama. Washington remained at Tuskegee until his death in 1915.

While fund-raising for Tuskegee, Washington traveled widely. His speeches caught the attention of politicians, educators, and newspaper editors. By the time he published his autobiography, *Up from Slavery*, in 1901, he had become the leading spokesman for America's black citizens.

In his speeches and writings, Washington pressed the Tuskegee mission: Black Americans must focus on finding an economic niche in turn-of-the-twentieth-century American society. Rather than agitating for political rights and social equality, African Americans should focus on industrial training; they should become tradesmen, farmers, nurses, and teachers. According to Washington, after proving themselves economically self-reliant and after positioning themselves as indispensable cogs in the American economy, black Americans would eventually be granted political and social equality.

Although Washington's message resonated with white Americans and with many blacks as well, he received a good deal of criticism from other black reformers. His most eloquent critic was W.E.B. DuBois, the Harvard-educated author of *The Souls of Black Folk*, published in 1903. DuBois and his followers criticized Washington for compromising with white America—for sacrificing political and social equality for economic opportunity.

The intense debate surrounding Washington and his message reveals that the generation of black reformers that emerged at the start of the twentieth century did not speak with a single voice. These reformers surely addressed a common core of social problems—education, employment, voting rights, social equality—but their approaches and solutions to these problems varied widely, resulting sometimes in tension and friction within the civil rights movement during the early twentieth century.

A New Era of Industrial Progress

Booker T. Washington

> On September 18, 1895, Booker T. Washington delivered his most famous speech, the Atlanta Exposition Address, which presented his vision for the role that blacks would play in the South's economy and culture. This excerpt from his autobiography, *Up from Slavery*, records the speech and the positive reaction that it received. Nonetheless, Washington's critics came to call the speech the Atlanta Compromise Address. Washington's detractors argued that he had offered the South an unpalatable compromise: Give Southern blacks educational and occupational opportunities and they will not agitate for political and social equality.

The Atlanta Exposition, at which I had been asked to make an address as a representative of the Negro race . . . was opened with a short address from Governor Bullock. After other interesting exercises, including an invocation from Bishop Nelson, of Georgia, a dedicatory ode by Albert Howell, Jr., and addresses by the President of the Exposition and Mrs. Joseph Thompson, the President of the Woman's Board, Governor Bullock introduced me with the words, "We have with us to-day a representative of Negro enterprise and Negro civilization."

When I arose to speak, there was considerable cheering, especially from the coloured people. As I remember it now, the thing that was uppermost in my mind was the desire to

Booker T. Washington, *Up from Slavery and Other Early Black Narratives*, New York: Doubleday, 1998.

say something that would cement the friendship of the races and bring about hearty coöperation between them. So far as my outward surroundings were concerned, the only thing that I recall distinctly now is that when I got up, I saw thousands of eyes looking intently into my face. The following is the address which I delivered:—

The Atlanta Exposition Address

Mr. President and Gentlemen of the Board of Directors and Citizens.

One-third of the population of the South is of the Negro race. No enterprise seeking the material, civil, or moral welfare of this section can disregard this element of our population and reach the highest success. I but convey to you, Mr. President and Directors, the sentiment of the masses of my race when I say that in no way have the value and manhood of the American Negro been more fittingly and generously recognized than by the managers of this magnificent Exposition at every stage of its progress. It is a recognition that will do more to cement the friendship of the two races than any occurrence since the dawn of our freedom.

Not only this, but the opportunity here afforded will awaken among us a new era of industrial progress. Ignorant and inexperienced, it is not strange that in the first years of our new life we began at the top instead of at the bottom; that a seat in Congress or the state legislature was more sought than real estate or industrial skill; that the political convention or stump speaking had more attractions than starting a dairy farm or truck garden.

A ship lost at sea for many days suddenly sighted a friendly vessel. From the mast of the unfortunate vessel was seen a signal, "Water, water; we die of thirst!" The answer from the friendly vessel at once came back, "Cast down your bucket where you are." A second time the signal, "Water, water; send us water!" ran up from the distressed vessel, and was answered, "Cast down your bucket where you are." And a third and fourth signal for water was answered, "Cast down your bucket where you are." The captain of the distressed vessel, at last heeding the injunction, cast down his bucket, and it came up full of fresh, sparkling water from the mouth of the Amazon River. To those of my race who depend on bettering their condition in a foreign land or who underestimate the importance of cultivating friendly relations with the Southern white man, who is their next-door neighbour, I would say: "Cast down your bucket where you are"—cast it down in making friends in every manly way of the people of all races by whom we are surrounded.

Focus on the Professions

Cast it down in agriculture, mechanics, in commerce, in domestic service, and in the professions. And in this connection it is well to bear in mind that whatever other sins the South may be called to bear, when it comes to business, pure and simple, it is in the South that the Negro is given a man's chance in the commercial world, and in nothing is this Exposition more eloquent than in emphasizing this chance. Our greatest danger is that in the great leap from slavery to freedom we may overlook the fact that the masses of us are to live by the productions of our hands, and fail to keep in mind that we shall prosper in proportion as we learn to dignify and glorify common labour and put brains and skill into the common occupations of life; shall prosper in proportion as we learn to draw the line between the superficial and the substantial, the ornamental gewgaws of life and the useful. No race can prosper till it learns that there is as much dignity in tilling a field as in writing a poem. It is at the bottom of life we must begin, and not at the top. Nor should we permit our grievances to overshadow our opportunities.

To those of the white race who look to the incoming of those of foreign birth and strange tongue and habits for the prosperity of the South, were I permitted I would repeat what I say to my own race, "Cast down your bucket where you are." Cast it down among the eight millions of Negroes whose habits you know, whose fidelity and love you have tested in days when to have proved treacherous meant the ruin of your firesides. Cast down your bucket among these people who have, without strikes and labour wars, tilled your fields, cleared your forests, builded your railroads and cities, and brought forth treasures from the bowels of the earth, and helped make possible this magnificent representation of the progress of the South. Casting down your bucket among my people, helping and encouraging them as you are doing on these grounds, and to education of head, hand, and heart, you will find that they will buy your surplus land, make blossom the waste places in your fields, and run your factories. While doing this, you can be sure in the future, as in the past, that you and your families will be surrounded by the most patient, faithful, law-abiding, and unresentful people that the world has seen. As we have proved

Washington advocated education and self-reliance. He believed that African Americans would find an equal place in society as they became more independent.

our loyalty to you in the past, in nursing your children, watching by the sick-bed of your mothers and fathers, and often following them with tear-dimmed eyes to their graves, so in the future, in our humble way, we shall stand by you with a devotion that no foreigner can approach, ready to lay down our lives, if need be, in defence of yours, interlacing our industrial, commercial, civil, and religious life with yours in a way that shall make the interests of both races one. In all things that are purely social we can be as separate as the fingers, yet one as the hand in all things essential to mutual progress.

Becoming a Useful Citizen

There is no defence or security for any of us except in the highest intelligence and development of all. If anywhere there are efforts tending to curtail the fullest growth of the Negro, let these efforts be turned into stimulating, encouraging, and making him the most useful and intelligent citizen. Effort or means so invested will pay a thousand per cent interest. These efforts will be twice blessed—"blessing him that gives and him that takes."

There is no escape through law of man or God from the inevitable:—

> The laws of changeless justice bind
>   Oppressor with oppressed;
> And close as sin and suffering joined
>   We march to fate abreast.

Nearly sixteen millions of hands will aid you in pulling the load upward, or they will pull against you the load downward. We shall constitute one-third and more of the ignorance and crime of the South, or one-third its intelligence and progress; we shall contribute one-third to the business and industrial prosperity of the South, or we shall prove a veritable body of death, stagnating, depressing, retarding every effort to advance the body politic.

Gentlemen of the Exposition, as we present to you our humble effort at an exhibition of our progress, you must not expect overmuch. Starting thirty years ago with ownership here and there in a few quilts and pumpkins and chickens (gathered from miscellaneous sources), remember the path that has led from these to the inventions and production of agricultural implements, buggies, steam-engines, newspapers, books, statuary, carving, paintings, the management of drugstores and banks, has not been trodden without contact with thorns and thistles. While we take pride in what we exhibit as a result of our independent efforts, we do not for a moment forget that our part in this exhibition would fall far short of your expectations but for the constant help that has come to our educational life, not only from the Southern states, but especially from Northern philanthropists, who have made their gifts a constant stream of blessing and encouragement.

Agitating for Social Equality Is Folly

The wisest among my race understand that the agitation of questions of social equality is the extremest folly, and that progress in the enjoyment of all the privileges that will come to us must be the result of severe and constant struggle rather than of artificial forcing. No race that has anything to contribute to the markets of the world is long in any degree ostracized. It is important and right that all privileges of the law be ours, but it is vastly more important that we be prepared for the exercises of these privileges. The opportunity to earn a dollar in a factory just now is worth infinitely more than the opportunity to spend a dollar in an opera-house.

In conclusion, may I repeat that nothing in thirty years has given us more hope and encouragement, and drawn us so near to you of the white race, as this opportunity offered by the Exposition; and here bending, as it were, over the altar that represents the results of the struggles of your race and mine, both starting practically empty-handed three decades ago, I pledge that in your effort to work out the great and intricate problem which God has laid at the doors of the South, you shall have at all times the patient, sympathetic help of my race; only let this be constantly in mind, that, while from representations in these buildings of the product of field, of forest, of mine, of factory, letters, and art, much good will come, yet far above and beyond material benefits will be that higher good, that, let us pray God, will come, in a blotting out of sectional differences and racial animosities and suspicions, in a determination to administer absolute justice, in a willing obedience among all classes to the mandates of law. This, this, coupled with our material prosperity, will bring into our beloved South a new heaven and a new earth.

Reactions to Washington's Address

The first thing that I remember, after I had finished speaking, was that Governor Bullock rushed across the platform and took me by the hand, and that others did the same. I received so many and such hearty congratulations that I found it difficult to get out of the building. I did not appreciate to any degree, however, the impression which my address seemed to have made, until the next morning, when I went into the business part of the city. As soon as I was recognized, I was surprised to find myself pointed out and surrounded by a crowd of men who wished to shake hands with me. This was kept up on every street on to which I went, to an extent which embarrassed me so much that I went back to my boarding-place. The next morning I returned to Tuskegee. At the station in Atlanta, and at almost all of the stations at which the train stopped between that city and Tuskegee, I found a crowd of people anxious to shake hands with me.

The papers in all parts of the United States published the address in full, and for months afterward there were complimentary editorial references to it. Mr. Clark Howell, the editor of the Atlanta *Constitution*, telegraphed to a New York paper, among other words, the following, "I do not exaggerate when I say that Professor Booker T. Washington's address yesterday was one of the most notable speeches, both as to character and as to the warmth of its reception, ever delivered to a Southern audience. The address was a revelation. The whole speech is a platform upon which blacks and whites can stand with full justice to each other."

The Boston *Transcript* said editorially: "The speech of Booker T. Washington at the Atlanta Exposition, this week, seems to have dwarfed all the other proceedings and the Exposition itself. The sensation that it has caused in the press has never been equalled."

I very soon began receiving all kinds of propositions from lecture bureaus, and editors of magazines and papers, to take the lecture platform, and to write articles. One lecture bureau offered me fifty thousand dollars, or two hundred dollars a night and expenses, if I would place my services at its disposal for a given period. To all these communications I replied that my life-work was at Tuskegee; and that whenever I spoke it must be in the interests of the Tuskegee school and my race, and that I would enter into no arrangements that seemed to place a mere commercial value upon my services.

Some days after its delivery I sent a copy of my address to the President of the United States, the Hon. Grover Cleveland. I received from him the following autograph reply:—

Gray Gables, Buzzard's Bay, Mass.,

October 6, 1895.

Booker T. Washington, Esq.:

My Dear Sir: I thank you for sending me a copy of your address delivered at the Atlanta Exposition.

I thank you with much enthusiasm for making the address. I have read it with intense interest, and I think the Exposition would be fully justified if it did not do more than furnish the opportunity for its delivery. Your words cannot fail to delight and encourage all who wish well for your race; and if our coloured fellow-citizens do not from your utterances gather new hope and form new determinations to gain every valuable advantage offered them by their citizenship, it will be strange indeed.

Yours very truly,

Grover Cleveland.

A Critique of Booker T. Washington's Message

W.E.B. DuBois

> William Edward Burghardt DuBois was born in Massachu-
> setts in 1868. He received his B.A. degree from Fisk Univer-
> sity and an M.A. and Ph.D. from Harvard. After completing
> his education, DuBois began a long academic career that took
> him to Wilberforce University, the University of Pennsylva-
> nia, and Atlanta University. DuBois became one of Booker T.
> Washington's sharpest critics. This excerpt from DuBois's
> masterwork, *The Souls of Black Folk*, published in 1903, pre-
> sents an eloquent critique of Washington's belief that civil
> rights for African Americans should be sacrificed—even tem-
> porarily—for economic development. In 1909, DuBois and
> his followers established the National Association for the
> Advancement of Colored People, a national organization that
> continues to advocate for racial equality for all Americans.
> DuBois spent his final years in Ghana, Africa, where he died
> in 1963.

Booker T. Washington arose as essentially the leader not of one race but of two,—a compromiser between the South, the North, and the Negro. Naturally the Negroes re-sented, at first bitterly, signs of compromise which surren-dered their civil and political rights, even though this was to be exchanged for larger chances of economic development.

W.E.B. DuBois, *The Souls of Black Folk*, New York: Penguin Books, 1989.

The rich and dominating North, however, was not only weary of the race problem, but was investing largely in Southern enterprises, and welcomed any method of peaceful coöperation. Thus, by national opinion, the Negroes began to recognize Mr. Washington's leadership; and the voice of criticism was hushed.

Mr. Washington represents in Negro thought the old attitude of adjustment and submission; but adjustment at such a peculiar time as to make his programme unique. This is an age of unusual economic development, and Mr. Washington's programme naturally takes an economic cast, becoming a gospel of Work and Money to such an extent as apparently almost completely to overshadow the higher aims of life. Moreover, this is an age when the more advanced races are coming in closer contact with the less developed races, and the race-feeling is therefore intensified; and Mr. Washington's programme practically accepts the alleged inferiority of the Negro races. Again, in our own land, the reaction from the sentiment of war time has given impetus to race-prejudice against Negroes, and Mr. Washington withdraws many of the high demands of Negroes as men and American citizens. In other periods of intensified prejudice all the Negro's tendency to self-assertion has been called forth; at this period a policy of submission is advocated. In the history of nearly all other races and peoples the doctrine preached at such crises has been that manly self-respect is worth more than lands and houses, and that a people who voluntarily surrender such respect, or cease striving for it, are not worth civilizing.

Washington's Faulty Arguments

In answer to this, it has been claimed that the Negro can survive only through submission. Mr. Washington distinctly asks that black people give up, at least for the present, three things,—

First, political power,
Second, insistence on civil rights,
Third, higher education of Negro youth,—

and concentrate all their energies on industrial education, the accumulation of wealth, and the conciliation of the South. This policy has been courageously and insistently advocated for over fifteen years, and has been triumphant for perhaps ten years. As a result of this tender of the palm-branch, what has been the return? In these years there have occurred:

1. The disfranchisement of the Negro.
2. The legal creation of a distinct status of civil inferiority for the Negro.
3. The steady withdrawal of aid from institutions for the higher training of the Negro.

These movements are not, to be sure, direct results of Mr. Washington's teachings; but his propaganda has, without a shadow of doubt, helped their speedier accomplishment. The question then comes: Is it possible, and probable, that nine millions of men can make effective progress in economic lines if they are deprived of political rights, made a servile caste, and allowed only the most meagre chance for developing their exceptional men? If history and reason give any distinct answer to these questions, it is an emphatic *No*. And Mr. Washington thus faces the triple paradox of his career:

1. He is striving nobly to make Negro artisans business men and property-owners; but it is utterly impossible, under modern competitive methods, for workingmen and property-owners to defend their rights and exist without the right of suffrage.
2. He insists on thrift and self-respect, but at the same time counsels a silent submission to civic inferiority such as is bound to sap the manhood of any race in the long run.
3. He advocates common-school and industrial training, and depreciates institutions of higher learning; but neither the Negro common-schools, nor Tuskegee itself, could remain open a day were it not for teachers trained in Negro colleges, or trained by their graduates.

This triple paradox in Mr. Washington's position is the object of criticism by two classes of colored Americans. One class is spiritually descended from Toussaint the Savior, through Gabriel, Vesey, and Turner, and they represent the attitude of revolt and revenge; they hate the white South blindly and distrust the white race generally, and so far as they agree on definite action, think that the Negro's only hope lies in emigration beyond the borders of the United States. And yet, by the irony of fate, nothing has more effectually made this programme seem hopeless than the recent course of the United States toward weaker and darker peoples in the West Indies, Hawaii, and the Philippines,—

Booker T. Washington on Slavery

Booker T. Washington was often criticized by other black reformers for not wholeheartedly condemning slavery. Washington stated his views on slavery in his autobiography Up from Slavery, *published in 1901.*

I pity from the bottom of my heart any nation or body of people that is so unfortunate as to get entangled in the net of slavery. I have long since ceased to cherish any spirit of bitterness against the Southern white people on account of the enslavement of my race. No one section of our country was wholly responsible for its introduction, and, besides, it was recognized and protected for years by the General Government. Having once got its tentacles fastened on to the economic and social life of the Republic, it was no easy matter for the country to relieve itself of the institution. Then, when we rid ourselves of prejudice, or racial feeling, and look facts in the face, we must acknowledge that, notwithstanding the cruelty and moral wrong of slavery, the ten million Negroes inhabiting this country, who themselves or their ancestors went through the school of American slavery, are in a stronger and more hopeful condition, materially, intellectually, morally, and religiously, than is true of an equal number of black people in any other position of the globe.

Booker T. Washington, *Up from Slavery and Other Early Black Narratives.* New York: Doubleday, 1998, p. 17.

for where in the world may we go and be safe from lying and brute force?

The other class of Negroes who cannot agree with Mr. Washington has hitherto said little aloud. They deprecate the sight of scattered counsels, of internal disagreement; and especially they dislike making their just criticism of a useful and earnest man an excuse for a general discharge of venom from small-minded opponents. Nevertheless, the questions involved are so fundamental and serious that it is difficult to see how men like the Grimkes, Kelly Miller, J.W.E. Bowen, and other representatives of this group, can much longer be silent. Such men feel in conscience bound to ask of this nation three things:

1. The right to vote.
2. Civic equality.
3. The education of youth according to ability. . . .

Dangerous Half-Truths

It would be unjust to Mr. Washington not to acknowledge that in several instances he has opposed movements in the South which were unjust to the Negro; he sent memorials to the Louisiana and Alabama constitutional conventions, he has spoken against lynching, and in other ways has openly or silently set his influence against sinister schemes and unfortunate happenings. Notwithstanding this, it is equally true to assert that on the whole the distinct impression left by Mr. Washington's propaganda is, first, that the South is justified in its present attitude toward the Negro because of the Negro's degradation; secondly, that the prime cause of the Negro's failure to rise more quickly is his wrong education in the past; and, thirdly, that his future rise depends primarily on his own efforts. Each of these propositions is a dangerous half-truth. The supplementary truths must never be lost sight of: first, slavery and race-prejudice are potent if not sufficient causes of the Negro's position; second, industrial and common-school training were necessarily slow in planting because they had to await the black teachers trained by higher institutions,—it being extremely doubtful if any essentially different development was possible, and certainly a Tuskegee was unthinkable before 1880; and, third, while it is a great truth to say that the Negro must strive and strive mightily to help himself, it is equally true that unless his striving be not simply seconded, but rather aroused and encouraged, by the initiative of the richer and wiser environing group, he cannot hope for great success.

In his failure to realize and impress this last point, Mr. Washington is especially to be criticised. His doctrine has tended to make the whites, North and South, shift the burden of the Negro problem to the Negro's shoulders and stand aside as critical and rather pessimistic spectators; when in fact the burden belongs to the nation, and the hands of none of us are clean if we bend not our energies to righting these great wrongs.

The South ought to be led, by candid and honest criticism, to assert her better self and do her full duty to the race she has cruelly wronged and is still wronging. The North—her co-partner in guilt—cannot salve her conscience by plastering it with gold. We cannot settle this problem by diplomacy and suaveness, by "policy" alone. If worse come to worst, can the moral fibre of this country survive the slow throttling and murder of nine millions of men?

The black men of America have a duty to perform, a duty stern and delicate,—a forward movement to oppose a part of the work of their greatest leader. So far as Mr. Washington preaches Thrift, Patience, and Industrial Training for the masses, we must hold up his hands and strive with him, rejoicing in his honors and glorying in the strength of this Joshua called of God and of man to lead the headless host. But so far as Mr. Washington apologizes for injustice, North or South, does not rightly value the privilege and duty of voting, belittles the emasculating effects of caste distinctions, and opposes the higher training and ambition of our brighter minds,—so far as he, the South, or the Nation, does this,—we must unceasingly and firmly oppose them. By every civilized and peaceful method we must strive for the rights which the world accords to men, clinging unwaveringly to those great words which the sons of the Fathers would fain forget: "We hold these truths to be self-evident: That all men are created equal; that they are endowed by their Creator with certain unalienable rights; that among these are life, liberty, and the pursuit of happiness."

Booker T. Washington's Accomplishments

Pauline Hopkins

> Pauline Hopkins, a native of Maine, became one of the most important African American editors of the turn of the twentieth century. In 1900, Hopkins became the contributing literary editor of *Colored American Magazine*, one of the most important African American periodicals of the era. For that magazine, Hopkins authored three serialized novels, historical articles, and short biographies of important African American citizens. Booker T. Washington was the subject of one of her biographical pieces. In that article, Hopkins pays tribute to Washington for his impressive achievements but also criticizes him for not urging the Federal government to address the South's racial problems. She left her post at the *Colored American Magazine* in 1904, perhaps because Washington began to influence the periodical's content at that time.

D r. Washington's public career as a speaker is full of interest: we can, of course, in an article like this, give but a bare outline of many brilliant occasions in which he has participated as the central figure. His speeches on the Negro problem, and in behalf of the Institute, are able and teem with humor, and they possess also the essential property of attracting the attention of the monied element, for Dr. Washington is without a peer in this particular line, and as a result

Pauline Hopkins, *The Norton Anthology of African American Literature*, edited by Henry Louis Gates Jr. and Nellie Y. McKay, New York: W.W. Norton, 1997.

Tuskegee is the richest Negro educational plant in the world.

Immediately after the public meeting held at the Hollis Street Theatre in 1899, friends quietly started a movement to raise a certain sum of money, to be used in sending Dr. and Mrs. Washington to Europe. They remained abroad from May 10 until August 5, gaining much needed rest. While [the Washingtons were] abroad lynching was especially frequent in the South, and Mr. Washington addressed a letter to the Southern people through the medium of the press. We give an excerpt:

Southern Solutions for Southern Problems

"With all the earnestness of my heart I want to appeal, not to the President of the United States, Mr. McKinley, not to the people of New York nor of the New England States, but to the citizens of our Southern States, to assist in creating a public sentiment such as will make human life here just as safe and sacred as it is anywhere else in the world.

"For a number of years the South has appealed to the North and to Federal authorities, through the public press, from the public platform and most eloquently through the late Henry W. Grady, to leave the whole matter of the rights and protection of the Negro to the South, declaring that it would see to it that the Negro would be made secure in his citizenship. During the last half dozen years the whole country, from the President down, has been inclined more than ever to pursue this policy, leaving the whole matter of the destiny of the Negro to the Negro himself and to the Southern white people among whom the great bulk of the Negroes live.

"By the present policy of non-interference on the part of the North and the Federal Government, the South is given a sacred trust. How will she execute this trust?" It is all very well to talk of the Negro's immorality and illiteracy, and that raising him out of the Slough of Despond will benefit the South and remove unpleasantness between the races, but until the same course is pursued with the immoral and illiterate *white* Southerner that is pursued with the Negro, there will be no peace in that section. Ignorance is as harmful in one race as in another. The South keeps on in her mad carnage of blood: she refuses to be conciliated. The influence and wealth which have flowed into Hampton and Tuskegee have awakened jealous spite. She doesn't care a rap for the "sacred trust" of Grady or any other man. We hear a lot of talk against the methods of the anti-slavery leaders, but no abolitionist ever used stronger language than the Rev. Quincy Ewing of Mississippi, in his recent great speech against lynching. We wonder how they like it down that way? Will they hang him or burn him?

The effect of that speech has been as electrical as was the first gun from Sumter [that began the Civil War]. We could shout for joy over the words: "I have always been and am now a States-right Democrat; but I say with no sort of hesitation that if Mississippi cannot put a stop to the lynching of Negroes within her borders—Negroes, let us remember, who are citizens of the United States as well as of Mississippi—then the Federal Government ought to take a hand in this business!" The reverend gentleman does not believe in treating a cancer with rose water.

Tuskegee's Accomplishments

Through the generosity of wealthy friends, Tuskegee has now an endowment fund of $150,000, from which the school is receiving interest.

The site of the Institute is now 835 acres. The other large tract is about four miles southeast of the Institute and is composed of 800 acres and known as "Marshall farm." Upon the home farm is located forty-two buildings. Of these, Alabama, Davidson, Huntington, Cassidy and Science Halls, the Agricultural Trades and Laundry Buildings, and the chapel are built of brick. There are also two large frame halls—Porter and Phelps Halls, small frame buildings and cottages used for commissary storerooms, recitation rooms, dormitories and teachers' residences. There are also the shop and saw-mill, with engine rooms and dynamo in conjunction. The brickyard, where the bricks needed in the construction of all brick buildings are made by pupils,

Tuskegee Institute students listen to a lecture on farm management. Booker T. Washington founded the institute in 1881.

turned out 1,500,000 bricks in 1899.

The Agricultural Department, Prof. G.W. Carver, of the Iowa State University, in charge, attracts much attention on account of changes wrought in old methods by scientific agriculture. The building is well-equipped at a cost of $10,000, and contains a fine chemical laboratory. Agriculture is an important feature in the life of the school. 135 acres of the home farm are devoted to raising vegetables, strawberries, grapes and other fruits. The Marshall farm is worked by student labor, keeping from thirty to forty-five boys on it constantly. It produces a large amount of the farm products used by the school and 800 head of live stock.

The Mechanical Department is in the Slater-Armstrong Memorial Trades' Building, dedicated in 1900. It is built entirely of brick, and contains twenty-seven rooms. The bricks were made by student labor. The building contains directors' office, reading room, exhibit room, wheelwright shop, blacksmith shop, tin shop, printing office, carpenter shop, repair shop, wood-working machine room, iron-working machine room, foundry, brick-making and plastering rooms, general stock and supply room, and a boiler and engine room. The second floor contains the mechanical drawing room, harness shop, paint shop, tailor shop, shoe shop, and electrical laboratory, and a room for carriage trimming and upholstering.

The Department of Domestic Science is directed by Mrs. Booker T. Washington, and embraces laundering, cooking, dressmaking, plain sewing, millinery and mattress making. A training school for nurses has for instructors the resident physician and a competent trained nurse.

There is also a division of music, a Bible training department and an academic department, all of which are carried on extensively with elaborate equipments.

From this brief review of the life of the founder of Tuskegee Institute and the prodigious growth of the work there we can but conclude that this is a phenomenal age in which we are living, and one of the most remarkable features of this age is Booker T. Washington,—his humble birth and rise to eminence and wealth.

View his career in whatever light we may, be we for or against his theories, his personality is striking, his life uncommon, and the magnetic influence which radiates from him in all direction, bending and swaying great minds and pointing the ultimate conclusion of colossal schemes as the wind the leaves of the trees, is stupendous. When the happenings of the Twentieth Century have become matters of history, Dr. Washington's motives will be open to as many constructions and discussions as are those of Napoleon today, or of other men of extraordinary ability, whether for good or evil, who have had like phenomenal careers.

Tensions Within the Civil Rights Movement

Ida B. Wells-Barnett

Ida B. Wells-Barnett, born a slave several months before the signing of the Emancipation Proclamation, became one of the leading African American reformers and civil rights activists during the Reconstruction era. After the Civil War, she attended Fisk University, where she learned the skills of journalism. She became a nationally known newspaper editor and columnist, and she used her position and reputation to advocate for civil rights for black Americans. Much of her civil rights activity focused on lynching, which had become widespread in the South after the Civil War. In this excerpt from her autobiography, which was published after her death in 1931, Wells-Barnett reveals some of the tensions present in the struggle for civil rights at the turn of the twentieth century. She describes the conflict between Booker T. Washington and W.E.B. DuBois, and she documents her own struggle for a leadership role in the movement for civil rights.

Not long after that [conference in Chicago] came a summons from New York, asking a conference of those who had signed the round robin which had been sent out in January. Following this a group of representative Negroes met in New York City in a three-day conference, deliberating on the form which our activities ought to take. It was

Ida B. Wells-Barnett, *Crusade for Justice: The Autobiography of Ida B. Wells*, edited by Alfreda M. Duster, Chicago, IL: University of Chicago Press, 1970. Copyright © 1931 by University of Chicago Press. Reproduced by permission.

called the National Negro Committee, although many white persons were present. There was an uneasy feeling that Mr. Booker T. Washington and his theories, which seemed for the moment to dominate the country, would prevail in the discussion as to what ought to be done.

Challenging Washington's Theories

Dr. Du Bois had written his *The Souls of Black Folk* the year following the fiasco of the Afro-American Council in Saint Paul. Although the country at large seemed to be accepting and adopting Mr. Washington's theories of industrial education, a large number agreed with Dr. Du Bois that it was impossible to limit the aspirations and endeavors of an entire race within the confines of the industrial education program.

Mr. Washington had a short time before held a conference of representative Negro men from all sections of the country, whose expenses had all been paid by some unknown person, and the feeling prevailed at our conference that an effort would be made to tie us to the chariot wheels of the industrial education program. Mr. Oswald Garrison Villard, the grandson of [abolitionist] William Lloyd Garrison, was very active in promoting our meeting. He had been an outspoken admirer of Mr. Washington, and the feeling seemed general that an endorsement of his industrial education would be the result.

Mr. Washington himself did not appear. But this feeling, like Banquo's ghost [in William Shakespeare's *Macbeth*], would not down. I was among those who tried to allay this feeling by asserting that most of those present were believers in Dr. Du Bois's ideas. It was finally decided that a committee of forty should be appointed to spend a year in devising ways and means for the establishment of an organization, and that we should come together the following year to hear its report. It was to be known as the National Negro Committee.

Forming the National Negro Committee

The subcommittee which had been appointed to recommend the names of persons to be on that committee included Dr.

Du Bois, who was the only Negro on it. It was also decided that the reading of that list should be the last thing done at the last session of our conference. Excitement bubbled over and warm speeches were made by William Monroe Trotter, editor of the *Guardian*, Boston, Massachusetts, Rev. R.C. Ransom, pastor of Bethel A.M.E. Church, New York City, Dr. J.W. Waldrom, pastor of the big Baptist church in Washington, D.C., and Dr. J.W. Mossell of Philadelphia and his good wife, Mrs. Gertrude Mossell.

Last but not least came T. Thomas Fortune and many others. They were all my personal friends, and I went from one to the other trying to allay the excitement, assuring them that their fears were groundless; that I had seen the list of names; that I had been elected as one, and that Mr. Washington's name was not only not on the list, but that mine was, along with others who were known to be opposed to the inclusiveness of Mr. Washington's industrial ideas.

When at last the moment arrived at which the committee was to make its report, Dr. Du Bois had been selected to read it. This was a compliment paid him by the white men who had been associated with him in the work, and I thought it gave notice of their approval of his plan and their disposition to stand by the program of those who believed that the Negro should be untrammeled in his efforts to secure higher education. Dr. Du Bois read the forty names chosen, and immediately after a motion to adopt was carried and the meeting adjourned.

Then bedlam broke loose; for although I had assured my friends that my name had been among those chosen, when Dr. Du Bois finished his list my name had not been called. I confess I was surprised, but I put the best face possible on the matter and turned to leave.

Tensions Within the Movement

Mr. John Milholland, a warm friend of the Negro . . . met me in the aisle as I was leaving the building and said, "Mrs. Barnett, I want to tell you that when that list of names left our hands and was given to Dr. Du Bois to read, your name led all the rest. It is unthinkable that you, who have fought the battle against lynching for nearly twenty years single-handed and alone when the rest of us were following our own selfish pursuits, should be left off such a committee."

I merely replied that it was very evident that someone did not want my presence on it, and that so far as I was concerned I would carry on just as I had done; that I was very glad that there was going to be a committee which would try to do something in a united and systematic way, because the work was far too large for any one person. As I reached the sidewalk on my way home, Miss May Nerney, the secretary, came running out and said, "Mrs. Barnett, they want you to come back."

The friend who was escorting me objected to my doing so, but finally consented to go back himself and see what was wanted. As I stood on the sidewalk waiting for his return, Miss Mary Ovington, who had taken active part in the deliberations, swept by me with an air of triumph and a very pleased look on her face. Mr. Harvey Thompson came back for me, and I returned to the building, where a great number of the friends were still discussing the personnel of that committee.

There were Mr. Milholland, Mr. William English Walling, Mr. Charles Edward Russell, and the other members of the committee who selected the names, all standing and awaiting my return. Dr. Du Bois was with them. He walked up to me and said, "Mrs. Barnett, I knew that you and Mr. Barnett were with Mrs. Wooley in the Douglass Center and that you would be represented through her. And I took the liberty of substituting the name of Dr. Charles E. Bentley for yours, Dr. Bentley to represent the Niagara Movement." "But," I said, "Dr. Bentley did not think enough of your movement to be present." "Well," he said, "nobody excepting those who were present in this room tonight knows that any change was made, and if you will consent I will go at once to the Associated Press office and have your name reinstated." I refused to permit him to do so. I told him that as he had done this purposely I was opposed to making any change.

Chapter 4

The Early Twentieth Century

Chapter Preface

D uring the first three decades of the twentieth century, black reformers focused on a number of issues that affected the lives of African American citizens. They attempted to raze the barriers that blocked black citizens from voting; they worked to extend to citizens of color equal protection of the laws; they promoted expanded educational and occupational opportunities for American blacks; and they fought to reform the segregated, so-called Jim Crow society that had developed in the American South in the wake of Reconstruction.

Despite the passage of the Fourteenth and Fifteenth Amendments to the U.S. Constitution in the aftermath of the Civil War, most black Americans, at the start of the twentieth century, lived as second-class citizens. In 1896, in the case of *Plessy v. Ferguson,* the U.S. Supreme Court ruled that state laws that mandated the separation of the races in public places were constitutional. In the South especially, these Jim Crow laws segregated public schools, parks and beaches, train stations and train cars, even public rest rooms. Many privately owned places of public accommodation, such as hotels and restaurants, did not serve black patrons or accepted them only in restricted seating.

Throughout the South, black citizens did not enjoy equal protection of the laws. Voting restrictions such as grandfather clauses (mandating that the children or grandchildren of slaves could not vote), literacy exams, and poll taxes kept blacks from the voting booths. Blacks who were arrested were often tried by all-white juries, convicted on the basis of flimsy evidence, and given harsher sentences than whites convicted of similar crimes. Thousands of African Americans charged with serious crimes were lynched without trial. Segregation laws and practices were enforced by the Ku Klux Klan.

During the opening decades of the twentieth century, millions of blacks fled the South to escape these harsh conditions. In the North, discrimination against black citizens was less overt, but northern blacks lacked educational and occupational opportunities. Few attended college. Most worked at jobs that afforded little opportunity for advancement. Black families lived in segregated neighborhoods, and their children attended inferior schools.

Black reformers of the early twentieth century attempted to address these issues. To some extent, these reformers were successful. A national antilynching campaign by the National Association for the Advancement of Colored People resulted in the passage of antilynching legislation in many states. A campaign to appeal the conviction of the Scottsboro Boys—nine black youths found guilty on insubstantial evidence of raping a white woman in Scottsboro, Alabama—resulted in an acquittal by the Supreme Court. Despite these victories, however, African Americans, on the eve of World War II, remained second-class citizens.

Fighting to Stop Lynching

Ida B. Wells-Barnett

> During the early decades of the twentieth century, Ida B.
> Wells-Barnett became involved with several issues that
> affected the lives of her fellow black citizens. The issue that
> received most of her attention was lynching—the execution
> without trial of black citizens accused of serious crimes. She
> became a tireless speaker and writer on this issue, meeting
> with and petitioning politicians to prevent an atrocity that
> took the lives of thousands of innocent blacks during the first
> three decades of the twentieth century. In this excerpt from
> her posthumously published life story, *Crusade for Justice:
> The Autobiography of Ida B. Wells*, Wells-Barnett describes
> her successful effort to remove from office the sheriff of
> Cairo, Illinois, for not preventing a lynching in his district.

Directly after the Springfield riot, at the next session of
the legislature, a law was enacted which provided that
any sheriff who permitted a prisoner to be taken from him
and lynched should be removed from office. This bill was
offered by Edward D. Green, who had been sent to Springfield to represent our race. Illinois had had not only a number of lynchings, but also a three days' riot at Springfield.

A Lynching in Cairo, Illinois

In due course of time the daily press announced that a
lynching had taken place in Cairo, Illinois. The body of a
white woman had been found in an alley in the residential

Ida B. Wells-Barnett, *Crusade for Justice: The Autobiography of Ida B. Wells*, edited by
Alfreda M. Duster, Chicago, IL: University of Chicago Press, 1970. Copyright © 1931 by
University of Chicago Press. Reproduced by permission.

THE EARLY TWENTIETH CENTURY

THE EARLY TWENTIETH CENTURY

THE EARLY TWENTIETH CENTURY   137

district and, following the usual custom, the police immediately looked for a Negro. Finding a shiftless, penniless colored man known as "Frog" James, who seemed unable to give a good account of himself, according to police, this man was locked up in the police station and according to the newspapers a crowd began to gather around the station and the sheriff was sent for.

Mr. Frank Davis, the sheriff, after a brief conversation with the prisoner, took him to the railroad station, got on the train, and took him up into the woods accompanied by a single deputy. They remained there overnight. Next morning, when a mob had grown to great proportions, they too went up into the country and had no trouble in locating the sheriff and his prisoner. He was placed on a train and brought back to town, accompanied by the sheriff. The newspapers announced that as the train came to a standstill, some of the mob put a rope around "Frog's" neck and dragged him out of the train and to the most prominent corner of the town, where the rope was thrown over an electric light arch and the body hauled up above the heads of the crowd.

Five hundred bullets were fired into it, some of which cut the rope, and the body dropped to the ground. Members of the mob seized hold of the rope and dragged the body up Washington Street, followed by men, women, and children, some of the women pushing baby carriages. The body was taken near to the place where the corpse of the white girl had been found. Here they cut off his head, stuck it on a fence post, built a fire around the body and burned it to a crisp.

Dismissing the Sheriff

When the news of this horrible thing appeared in the papers, immediately a meeting was called and a telegram sent to Governor Deneen demanding that the sheriff of Alexander County be dispossessed. The newspapers had already quoted the governor as saying that he did not think it mandatory on him to displace the sheriff. But when our telegram reached him calling attention to the law, he immediately ousted him by telegram.

This same law provided that after the expiration of a short time, the sheriff would have the right to appear before the governor and show cause why he ought to be reinstated. We had a telegram from Governor Deneen informing us that on the following Wednesday the sheriff would appear before him demanding reinstatement. Mr. Barnett spent some time urging representative men of our race to appear before the governor and fight the sheriff's reinstatement. . . .

A Trip to Cairo

I reached Cairo after nightfall, and was driven to the home of the leading A.M.E. [African Methodist Episcopal] minister, just before he went into church for his evening service. I told him why I was there and asked if he could give me any help in getting the sentiment of the colored people and investigating facts. He said that they all believed that "Frog" James had committed that murder. I asked him if he had anything upon which to base that belief. "Well," he said, "he was a worthless sort of fellow, just about the kind of a man who would do a trick like that. Anyhow, all of the colored people believe that and many of us have written letters already to the governor asking the reinstatement of the sheriff."

I sprang to my feet and asked him if he realized what he had done in condoning the horrible lynching of a fellowman who was a member of his race. Did he not know that if they condoned the lynching of one man, the time might come when they would have to condone that of other men higher up, providing they were black?

I asked him if he could direct me to the home of some other colored persons; that I had been sent to see all of them, and it wouldn't be fair for me to accept reports from one man alone. He gave me the names of one or two others, and I withdrew. I had expected to stop at his home, but after he told me that I had no desire to do so. One of the men named was Will Taylor, a druggist, whom I had known in Chicago, and I asked to be directed to his place. The minister's wife went with me because it was dark.

Mr. Taylor greeted me very cordially and I told him what

my mission was. He also secured me a stopping place with persons by the name of Lewis, whom I afterward found were teachers in the colored high schools, both the man and his wife. They welcomed me very cordially and listened to my story. I told them why I was there; they gave me a bed. The next morning Mrs. Lewis came and informed me that she had already telephoned Dr. Taylor that she was sorry she could not continue to keep me. I found afterward that after they heard the story they felt that discretion was the better part of valor.

Rallying Local Citizens

Mr. Taylor and I spent the day talking with colored citizens and ended with a meeting that night. I was driven to the place where the body of the murdered girl had been found, where the Negro had been burned, and saw about twenty-five representative colored people of the town that day. Many of those whom I found knew nothing whatever of the action that had been taken by the citizens of Chicago.

The meeting was largely attended and in my statement to them I said I had come down to be their mouthpiece; that I correctly understood how hard it would be for those who lived there to take an active part in the movement to oust the sheriff; that we were willing to take the lead in the matter but they must give me the facts; that it would be endangering the lives of other colored people in Illinois if we did not take a stand against the all too frequent lynchings which were taking place.

I went on to say that I came because I knew that they knew of my work against lynching for fifteen years past and felt that they would talk more freely to me and trust me more fully than they would someone of whom they knew nothing. I wanted them to tell me if Mr. Frank Davis had used his great power to protect the victim of the mob; if he had at any time placed him behind bars of the county jail as the law required; and if he had sworn in any deputies to help protect his prisoner as he was obliged by law to do until such time as he could be tried by due process of law. Although the meeting lasted for two hours, and although most of those present and speaking were friends of Frank Davis, some of whom had been deputy sheriffs in his office, not one of them could honestly say that Frank Davis had put his prisoner in the county jail or had done anything to protect him. I therefore offered a resolution to that effect which was almost unanimously adopted. There was one single objection by the ubiquitous "Uncle Tom" Negro who seems always present. I begged the people, if they could do nothing to help the movement to punish Frank Davis for such glaring negligence of his duty, that they would do nothing to hinder us.

Next morning before taking the train I learned of a Baptist ministers' meeting that was being held there and decided to attend for the purpose of having them pass the same resolution. I was told that it would do no good to make the effort and that it would delay me until midnight getting into Springfield.

Ida B. Wells-Barnett

But I went, got an opportunity to speak, offered the resolution, told of the men who had sent letters to the governor, showed how that would confuse his mind as to the attitude of the colored people on the subject, and stated clearly that all such action would mean that we would have other lynchings in Illinois whenever it suited the mob anywhere.

I asked the adoption of the resolution passed the night before. There was discussion pro and con, and finally the moderator arose and said, "Brethren, they say an honest confession is good for the soul. I, too, am one of those men who have written to the governor asking Frank Davis's reinstatement. I knew he was a friend of ours; that the man who had taken his place has turned out all Negro deputies and put in Democrats, and I was told that when the mob placed the rope around "Frog" James's neck the sheriff tried to prevent them and was knocked down for his pains. But now that the sister has shown us plainly the construction that would be placed upon that letter, I want her when she appears before the governor tomorrow to tell him that I take that letter back and hereby sign my name to this resolution." By this time the old man was shedding tears. Needless to say the resolution went through without any further objections.

Appealing to the Governor

Mr. Barnett had told me that he would prepare a brief based upon what had been gleaned from the daily press, which would be in the post office at Springfield when I got there Wednesday morning; that if I found any facts contrary to those mentioned I could easily make the correction. There had been no precedent for this procedure, but he assumed that the attorney general would be present to represent the people.

When I entered the room at ten o'clock that morning I looked around for some of my own race, thinking that perhaps they would journey to Springfield for the hearing, even though they had been unwilling to go to Cairo to get the facts. Not a Negro face was in evidence! On the other side of the room there was Frank Davis, and with him one of the biggest lawyers in southern Illinois, so I was afterward told, who was also a state senator.

There was the parish priest, the state's attorney of Alexander County, the United States land commissioner, and about half a dozen other representative white men who had journeyed from Cairo to give aid and comfort to Frank Davis in his fight for reinstatement.

The governor said that they had no precedent and that he would now hear the plea to be made by the sheriff; whereupon this big lawyer proceeded to present his petition for reinstatement and backed it up with letters and telegrams from Democrats and Republicans, bankers, lawyers, doctors, editors of both daily papers, and heads of women's clubs and of men's organizations. The whole of the white population of Cairo was evidently behind Frank Davis and his demand for reinstatement. . . .

Barnett States Her Case

When the gentlemen had finished, Governor Deneen said, "I understand Mrs. Barnett is here to represent the colored people of Illinois." Not until that moment did I realize that the burden depended upon me. . . .

I began by reading the brief which Mr. Barnett prepared in due legal form. I then launched out to tell of my investigation in Cairo. Before I had gotten very far the clock struck twelve, and Springfield being a country town, everything stopped so people could go home to dinner, which was served in the middle of the day. . . .

At two o'clock . . . we went back to the Capitol. I resumed the statement of facts I had found—of the meeting held Monday night and of the resolution passed there which stated Frank Davis had not put his prisoner in the county jail or sworn in deputies to protect him although he knew there was talk of mob violence.

I was interrupted at this point by Mr. Davis's lawyer. "Who wrote that resolution?" he asked. "Don't answer him," said Mr. Williams, "he is only trying to confuse you." "Isn't it a fact," said Mr. Davis's counsel, "that you wrote that resolution?" "Yes," I said, "I wrote the resolution and presented it, but the audience adopted and passed it. It was done in the same way as the petition which you have presented here. Those petitions were signed by men, but they were typewritten and worded by somebody who was interested enough in Mr. Davis to place them where the men could reach them. But that is not all, Governor; I have here the signature of that leading Baptist minister who has been so highly praised to you. I went to his meeting yesterday and when I told him what a mistake it was to seem to condone the outrage on a human being by writing a letter asking for the reinstatement of a man who permitted it to be done, he rose and admitted he had sent the letter which has been read in your hearing, but having realized his mistake he wanted me to tell you that he endorsed the resolutions which I have here, and here is his name signed to them."

And then I wound up by saying, "Governor, the state of Illinois has had too many terrible lynchings within her borders within the last few years. If this man is sent back it will be an encouragement to those who resort to mob violence and will do so at any time, well knowing they will not be called to account for so doing. All the colored friends in Cairo are friends of Mr. Davis and they seem to feel that because his successor, a Democrat, has turned out all the Republican deputies, they owe their duty to the party to ask the return of a Republican sheriff. But not one of these, Mr. Davis's friends, would say that for one moment he had his prisoner in the county jail where the law demands that he should be placed or that he swore in a single deputy to help protect his life until he could be tried by law. It looked like encouragement to the mob to have the chief law officer in the county take that man up in the woods and keep him until the mob got big enough to come after him. I repeat, Governor, that if this man is reinstated, it will simply mean an increase of lynchings in the state of Illinois and an encouragement to mob violence.". . .

Victory

The following Tuesday morning Governor Deneen issued one of the finest state papers that emanated from him during his whole eight years in the Capitol. The summary of his proclamation was that Frank Davis could not be reinstated because he had not properly protected the prisoner within his keeping and that lynch law could have no place in Illinois.

That was in 1909, and from that day until the present there has been no lynching in the state. Every sheriff, whenever there seem to be any signs of the kind, immediately telegraphs the governor for troops. And to Governor Deneen belongs the credit.

The Social Equality of Blacks and Whites

W.E.B. DuBois

In 1910, W.E.B. DuBois became the editor of *The Crisis*, the official publication of the National Association for the Advancement of Colored People (NAACP). DuBois used his position to articulate his views on racial issues in the United States. In this editorial, which originally appeared in the November 1920 issue of *Crisis*, DuBois takes up the topics of social equality and interracial marriage; he tries to clarify the NAACP's position on social equality, which he believes has been misunderstood by white Americans.

When The National Association for the Advancement of Colored People was organized it seemed to us that the subject of "social equality" between races was not one that we need touch officially whatever our private opinions might be. We announced clearly our object as being the political and civil rights of Negroes and this seemed to us a sufficiently clear explanation of our work.

We soon found, however, certain difficulties: Was the right to attend a theatre a civil or a social right? Is a hotel a private or a public institution? What should be our stand as to public travel or public celebrations or public dinners to discuss social uplift? And above all, should we be silent when laws were proposed taking away from a white father all legal responsibility for his colored child?

Moreover, no matter what our attitude, acts and clear

W.E.B. DuBois, *The Oxford W.E.B. DuBois Reader*, edited by Eric J. Sundquist, New York: Oxford University Press, 1996.

statements have been, we were continually being "accused" of advocating "social equality" and back of the accusations were implied the most astonishing assumptions: our secretary was assaulted in Texas for "advocating social equality" when in fact he was present to prove that we were a legal organization under Texas law. Attempts were made in North Carolina to forbid a state school from advertising in our organ THE CRISIS on the ground that "now and then it injects a note of social equality" and in general we have seen theft, injustice, lynchings, riot and murder based on "accusations" or attempts at "social equality."

Defining Social Equality

The time has, therefore, evidently come for THE CRISIS to take a public stand on this question in the interest of Justice and clear thinking. Let us openly define our terms and beliefs and let there be no further unjustifiable reticence on our part or underground skulking by enemies of the Negro race. This statement does not imply any change of attitude on our part; it simply means a clear and formal expression on matters which hitherto we have mistakenly assumed were unimportant in their relation to our main work.

We make this statement, too, the more willingly because recent events lead us to realize that there lurks in the use and the misuse of the phrase "social equality" much of the same virus that for thousands of years has separated and insulted and injured men of many races and groups and social classes.

We believe that social equality, by a reasonable interpretation of the words, means moral, mental and physical fitness to associate with one's fellowmen. In this sense THE CRISIS believes absolutely in the Social Equality of the Black and White and Yellow races and it believes too that any attempt to deny this equality by law or custom is a blow at Humanity, Religion and Democracy.

The Right to Mingle

No sooner is this incontestable statement made, however, than many minds immediately adduce further implications:

they say that such a statement and belief implies the right of black folk to force themselves into the private social life of whites and to intermarry with them.

This is a forced and illogical definition of social equality. Social equals, even in the narrowest sense of the term, do not have the *right* to be invited to, or attend private receptions, or to marry persons who do not wish to marry them. Such a right would imply not mere equality—it would mean superiority. Such rights inhere in reigning monarchs in certain times and countries, but no man, black or white, ever dreamed of claiming a right to invade the private social life of any man.

On the other hand, every self-respecting person does claim the right to mingle with his fellows *if he is invited* and to be free from insult or hindrance because of his presence. When, therefore, the public is invited, or when he is privately invited to social gatherings, the Negro has a right to accept and no other guest has a right to complain: they have only the right to absent themselves. The late Booker T. Washington could hardly be called an advocate of "social equality" in any sense and yet he repeatedly accepted invitations to private and public functions and certainly had the right to.

To the question of intermarriage there are three aspects:
1. The individual right
2. The social expediency
3. The physical result

The Question of Interracial Marriage

As to the individual right of any two sane grown individuals of any race to marry there can be no denial in any civilized land. The moral results of any attempt to deny this right are too terrible and of this the southern United States is an awful and abiding example. Either white people and black people want to mingle sexually or they do not. If they do, no law will stop them and attempted laws are cruel, inhuman and immoral. If they do not, no laws are necessary.

But above the individual problem lies the question of the

social expediency of the intermarriage of whites and blacks today in America. The answer to this is perfectly clear: it is not socially expedient today for such marriages to take place; the reasons are evident: where there are great differences of ideal, culture, taste and public esteem, the intermarriage of groups is unwise because it involves too great a strain to evolve a compatible, agreeable family life and to train up proper children. On this point there is almost complete agreement among colored and white people and the strong opinion here is not only that of the whites—it is the growing determination of the blacks to accept no alliances so long as there is any shadow of condescension; and to build a great black race tradition of which the Negro and the world will be as proud in the future as it has been in the ancient world.

THE CRISIS, therefore, most emphatically advises against race intermarriage in America but it does so while maintaining the moral and legal right of individuals who may think otherwise and it most emphatically refuses to base its opposition on other than social grounds.

THE CRISIS does not believe, for instance, that the intermarriage of races is physically criminal or deleterious. The overwhelming weight of scientific opinion and human experience is against this assumption and it is a cruel insult to seek to transmute a perfectly permissible social taste or thoughtful social advice into a confession or accusation of physical inferiority and contamination.

To sum up then: THE CRISIS advises strongly against interracial marriage in the United States today because of social conditions and prejudice and not for physical reasons; at the same time it maintains absolute legal right of such marriage for such as will, for the simple reason that any other solution is immoral and dangerous.

THE CRISIS does not for a moment believe that any man has a right to force his company on others in their private lives but it maintains just as strongly that the right of any man to associate privately with those who wish to associate with him and publicly with anybody so long as he conducts himself gently, is the most fundamental right of a Human Being.

Creating a Separate Black Nation

Marcus Garvey

Marcus Garvey was born in Jamaica in 1887 and migrated, as a young man, to New York, where he became intrigued with the idea of creating a separate, economically independent black society, either within American society or in Africa. He opposed the presence of European powers in Africa and took issue with African American reformers who believed that blacks could attain their civil rights and gain economic power in an integrated American society. Garvey's separatist views led to clashes with African American civil rights leaders such as W.E.B. DuBois. During the early 1920s, Garvey founded the Universal Negro Improvement Association and several business ventures—the Black Star Line (a shipping company) and the New Factories Corporation (an organization that promoted black-owned businesses)—to achieve his goals. In 1923, he was indicted and convicted of mail fraud and deported to Jamaica, which curbed his short but dynamic career as a black nationalist leader. This excerpt from an article that appeared in the September 1923 issue of *Current History* magazine explains the source of his separatist views and the difficulty that he has encountered in advocating them.

I was born in the Island of Jamaica, British West Indies, on August 17, 1887. My parents were black Negroes. My father was a man of brilliant intellect and dashing courage. He was unafraid of consequences. He took human chances

Marcus Garvey, *Philosophy and Opinions of Marcus Garvey*, edited by Amy Jacques Garvey, London: Frank Cass, 1967.

in the course of life, as most bold men do, and he failed at the close of his career. He once had a fortune; he died poor. My mother was a sober and conscientious Christian, too soft and good for the time in which she lived. She was the direct opposite of my father. He was severe, firm, determined, bold and strong, refusing to yield even to superior forces if he believed he was right. My mother, on the other hand, was always willing to return a smile for a blow, and ever ready to bestow charity upon her enemy. Of this strange combination I was born thirty-six years ago, and ushered into a world of sin, the flesh and the devil.

Childhood Years

I grew up with other black and white boys. I was never whipped by any, but made them all respect the strength of my arms. I got my education from many sources—through private tutors, two public schools, two grammar or high schools and two colleges. My teachers were men and women of varied experiences and abilities; four of them were eminent preachers. They studied me and I studied them. With some I became friendly in after years; others and I drifted apart, because as a boy they wanted to whip me, and I simply refused to be whipped. I was not made to be whipped. It annoys me to be defeated; hence to me, to be once defeated is to find cause for an everlasting struggle to reach the top.

I became a printer's apprentice at an early age, while still attending school. My apprentice master was a highly educated and alert man. In the affairs of business and the world he had no peer. He taught me many things before I reached twelve, and at fourteen I had enough intelligence and experience to manage men. I was strong and manly, and I made them respect me. I developed a strong and forceful character, and have maintained it still.

To me, at home in my early days, there was no difference between white and black. One of my father's properties, the place where I lived most of the time, was adjoining that of a white man. He had three girls and two boys; the Wesleyan minister, another white man, whose church my parents attended, also had property adjoining ours. He had three girls and one boy. All of us were playmates. We romped and were happy children, playmates together. The little white girl whom I liked most knew no better than I did myself. We were two innocent fools who never dreamed of a race feeling and problem. As a child, I went to school with white boys and girls, like all other Negroes. We were not called Negroes then. I never heard the term Negro used once until I was about fourteen.

Learning Racial Distinctions

At fourteen my little white playmate and I parted. Her parents thought the time had come to separate us and draw the color line. They sent her and another sister to Edinburgh, Scotland, and told her that she was never to write or try to get in touch with me, for I was a "nigger." It was then that I found for the first time that there was some difference in humanity, and that there were different races, each having its own separate and distinct social life. I did not care about the separation after I was told about it, because I never thought all during our childhood association that the girl and the rest of the children of her race were better than I was; in fact, they used to look up to me. So I simply had no regrets.

After my first lesson in race distinction, I never thought of playing with white girls any more, even if they might be next-door neighbors. At home my sisters' company was good enough for me, and at school I made friends with the colored girls next to me. White boys and I used to frolic together. We played cricket and baseball, ran races and rode bicycles together, took each other to the river and to the sea beach to learn to swim, and made boyish efforts while out in deep water to drown each other, making a sprint for shore crying out "Shark, shark, shark!" In all our experiences, however, only one black boy was drowned. He went under on a Friday afternoon after school hours, and his parents found him afloat, half eaten by sharks, on the following Sunday afternoon. Since then we boys never went sea bathing.

Realizing Racial Injustice

At maturity the black and white boys separated, and took different courses in life. I grew then to see the difference between the races more and more. My schoolmates as young men did not know or remember me any more. Then I realized that I had to make a fight for a place in the world, that it was not so easy to pass on to office and position. Personally, however, I had not much difficulty in finding and holding a place for myself, for I was aggressive. At eighteen I had an excellent position as manager of a large printing establishment, having under my control several men old enough to be my grandfathers. But I got mixed up with public life. I started to take an interest in the politics of my country, and then I saw the injustice done to my race because it was black, and I became dissatisfied on that account. I went traveling to South and Central America and parts of the West Indies to find out if it was so elsewhere, and I found the same situation. I set sail for Europe to find out if it was different there, and again I found the stumbling block—"You are black." I read of the conditions in America. I read "Up from Slavery," by Booker T. Washington, and then my doom—if I may so call it—of being a race leader dawned upon me in London after I had traveled through almost half of Europe.

I asked: "Where is the black man's Government?" "Where is his King and his kingdom?" "Where is his President, his country, and his ambassador, his army, his navy, his men of big affairs?" I could not find them, and then I declared, "I will help to make them."

Establishing the Universal Negro Improvement Association

Becoming naturally restless for the opportunity of doing something for the advancement of my race, I was determined that the black man would not continue to be kicked about by all the other races and nations of the world, as I saw it in the West Indies, South and Central America and

Europe, and as I read of it in America. My young and ambitious mind led me into flights of great imagination. I saw before me then, even as I do now, a new world of black men, not peons, serfs, dogs and slaves, but a nation of sturdy men making their impress upon civilization and causing a new light to dawn upon the human race. I could not remain in London any more. My brain was afire. There was a world of thought to conquer. I had to start ere it became too late and the work be not done. Immediately I boarded a ship at Southampton for Jamaica, where I arrived on July 15, 1914. The Universal Negro Improvement Association and African Communities (Imperial) League was founded and organized five days after my arrival, with the program of uniting all the Negro peoples of the world into one great body to establish a country and Government absolutely their own. . . .

This organization has succeeded in organizing the Negroes all over the world, and we now look forward to a renaissance that will create a new people and bring about the restoration of Ethiopia's ancient glory.

Being black, I have committed an unpardonable offense against the very light-colored Negroes in America and the West Indies by making myself famous as a Negro leader of millions. In their view, no black man must rise above them, but I still forge ahead determined to give to the world the truth about the new Negro who is determined to make and hold for himself a place in the affairs of men. The Universal Negro Improvement Association has been misrepresented by my enemies. They have tried to make it appear that we are hostile to other races. This is absolutely false. We love all humanity. We are working for the peace of the world, which we believe can only come about when all races are given their due.

The Views of the Improvement Association

We feel that there is absolutely no reason why there should be any differences between the black and white races, if each stop to adjust and steady itself. We believe in the purity of both races. We do not believe the black man should be encouraged in the idea that his highest purpose in life is to marry a white woman, and we do believe that the white man should be taught to respect the black woman in the same way as he wants the black man to respect the white woman. It is a vicious and dangerous doctrine of social equality to urge, as certain colored leaders do, that black and white should get together, for that would destroy the racial purity of both.

We believe that the black people should have a country of their own, where they should be given the fullest opportunity to develop politically, socially and industrially. The black people should not be encouraged to remain in white people's countries and expect to be Presidents, Governors, Mayors, Senators, Congressmen, Judges and social and industrial leaders. We believe that with the rising ambition of the Negro, if a country is not provided for him in another 50 or 100 years, there will be a terrible clash that will end disastrously to him and disgrace our civilization. We desire to prevent such a clash by pointing the Negro to a home of his own. We feel that all well-disposed and broad-minded white men will aid in this direction. It is because of this belief no doubt that my Negro enemies, so as to prejudice me further in the opinion of the public, wickedly state that I am a member of the Ku Klux Klan, even though I am a black man.

Dealing with the Opposition

I have been deprived of the opportunity of properly explaining my work to the white people of America, through the prejudice worked up against me by jealous and wicked members of my own race. My success as an organizer was much more than rival Negro leaders could tolerate. They, regardless of consequences, either to me or to the race, had to destroy me by fair means or foul. The thousands of anonymous and other hostile letters written to the editors and publishers of the white press by Negro rivals to prejudice me in the eyes of public opinion are sufficient evidence of the wicked and vicious opposition I have had to meet from among my own people, especially among the very light colored. But they went further than the press in their attempts to discredit me. They organized clubs all over the United States and the West Indies, and wrote both open and anonymous letters to city, State and Federal officials of this and other Governments to induce them to use their influence to hamper and destroy me. No wonder, therefore, that several Judges, District Attorneys and other high officials have been opposing me without knowing me. No wonder, therefore, that the great white population of this country and of the world has a wrong impression of the aims and objects of the Universal Negro Improvement Association and of the work of Marcus Garvey.

Having had the wrong education as a start in his racial career, the Negro has become his greatest enemy. Most of the trouble I have had in advancing the cause of the race has come from Negroes. Booker Washington aptly described the race in one of his lectures by stating that we were like crabs in a barrel, that none would allow the other to climb over, but on any such attempt all would continue to pull back into the barrel the one crab that would make the effort to climb out. Yet, those of us with vision cannot desert the race, leaving it to suffer and die.

Looking to the Future

Looking forward a century or two, we can see an economic and political death struggle for the survival of the different race groups. Many of our present-day national centres will have become overcrowded with vast surplus populations. The fight for bread and position will be keen and severe. The weaker and unprepared group is bound to go under. That is why, visionaries as we are in the Universal Negro Improvement Association, we are fighting for the founding of a Negro nation in Africa, so that there will be no clash between black and white and that each race will have a separate existence and civilization all its own without courting suspicion and hatred or eyeing each other with jealousy and rivalry within the borders of the same country.

White men who have struggled for and built up their

countries and their own civilizations are not disposed to hand them over to the Negro, or any other race, without let or hindrance. It would be unreasonable to expect this. Hence any vain assumption on the part of the Negro to imagine that he will one day become President of the Nation, Governor of the State, or Mayor of the City in the countries of white men, is like waiting on the devil and his angels to take up their residence in the Realm on high and direct there the affairs of Paradise.

Fleeing the South

Richard Wright

Richard Wright, born on a Mississippi plantation in 1908, became one of the most prominent African American fiction writers of the twentieth century. His fiction includes the story collections *Uncle Tom's Children*, published in 1938, and *Eight Men*, published in 1961, the year after Wright's death, and the blockbuster novel *Native Son*, published in 1940. His fictional works generally depict black characters frustrated with life in twentieth-century America. Wright also presented his views on America's racial dilemmas in nonfiction works such as *Twelve Million Black Voices*, published in 1941, and in essays that appeared in *New Masses* and *The Atlantic Monthly*. In this excerpt from his autobiography *Black Boy*, published in 1945, Wright explains that he could not achieve his goal of becoming a writer without leaving the rigidly segregated South and heading North, which he did at age nineteen.

I dreamed of going north and writing books, novels. The North symbolized to me all that I had not felt and seen; it had no relation whatever to what actually existed. Yet, by imagining a place where everything was possible, I kept hope alive in me. But where had I got this notion of doing something in the future, of going away from home and accomplishing something that would be recognized by others? I had, of course, read my Horatio Alger stories, my pulp stories, and I knew my Get-Rich-Quick Wallingford series from cover to cover, though I had sense enough not to hope to get rich; even to my naïve imagination that possibility was too remote. I knew that I lived in a country in which the aspirations of black people were limited, marked-off. Yet I felt that I had to go somewhere and do something to redeem my being alive.

Building a Dream

I was building up in me a dream which the entire educational system of the South had been rigged to stifle. I was feeling the very thing that the state of Mississippi had spent millions of dollars to make sure that I would never feel; I was becoming aware of the thing that the Jim Crow laws had been drafted and passed to keep out of my consciousness; I was acting on impulses that southern senators in the nation's capital had striven to keep out of Negro life; I was beginning to dream the dreams that the state had said were wrong, that the schools had said were taboo.

Had I been articulate about my ultimate aspirations, no doubt someone would have told me what I was bargaining for; but nobody seemed to know, and least of all did I. My classmates felt that I was doing something that was vaguely wrong, but they did not know how to express it. As the outside world grew more meaningful, I became more concerned, tense; and my classmates and my teachers would say: "Why do you ask so many questions?" Or: "Keep quiet."

I was in my fifteenth year; in terms of schooling I was far behind the average youth of the nation, but I did not know that. In me was shaping a yearning for a kind of consciousness, a mode of being that the way of life about me had said could not be, must not be, and upon which the penalty of death had been placed. Somewhere in the dead of the southern night my life had switched onto the wrong track and, without my knowing it, the locomotive of my heart was rushing down a dangerously steep slope, heading for a collision, heedless of the warning red lights that blinked all about me, the sirens and the bells and the screams that filled the air. . . .

I knew what was wrong with me, but I could not correct it. The words and actions of white people were baffling signs to me. I was living in a culture and not a civilization and I could learn how that culture worked only by living with it. Misreading the reactions of whites around me made me say and do the wrong things. In my dealing with whites I was conscious of the entirety of my relations with them, and they were conscious only of what was happening at a given moment. I had to keep remembering what others took for granted; I had to think out what others felt.

I had begun coping with the white world too late. I could not make subservience an automatic part of my behavior. I had to feel and think out each tiny item of racial experience in the light of the whole race problem, and to each item I brought the whole of my life. While standing before a white man I had to figure out how to perform each act and how to say each word. I could not help it. I could not grin. In the past I had always said too much, now I found that it was difficult to say anything at all. I could not react as the world in which I lived expected me to; that world was too baffling, too uncertain.

I was idle for weeks. The summer waned. Hope for school was now definitely gone. Autumn came and many of the boys who held jobs returned to school. Jobs were now numerous. I heard that hallboys were needed at one of the hotels, the hotel in which Ned's brother had lost his life. Should I go there? Would I, too, make a fatal slip? But I had to earn money. I applied and was accepted to mop long white tiled hallways that stretched around the entire perimeter of the office floors of the building. I reported each night at ten, got a huge pail of water, a bushel of soap flakes and, with a gang of moppers, I worked. All the boys were Negroes and I was happy; at least I could talk, joke, laugh, sing, say what I pleased.

I began to marvel at how smoothly the black boys acted out the roles that the white race had mapped out for them. Most of them were not conscious of living a special, separate, stunted way of life. Yet I knew that in some period of their growing up—a period that they had no doubt forgotten—there had been developed in them a delicate, sensitive controlling mechanism that shut off their minds and emotions from all that the white race had said was taboo. Although they lived in an America where in theory there existed equality of opportunity, they knew unerringly what to aspire to and what not to aspire to. Had a black boy announced that he aspired to be a writer, he would have been unhesitatingly called crazy by his pals. Or had a black boy

The Great Black Migration

During the first three decades of the twentieth century, millions of Southern blacks left the South and headed North, into the large cities where jobs were available. Richard Wright documents this Great Black Migration in Twelve Million Black Voices, *published in 1941. This excerpt from that book suggests that the North was not the longed-for promised land for most blacks who left the South.*

Perhaps never in history has a more utterly unprepared folk wanted to go to the city; we were barely born as a folk when we headed for the tall and sprawling centers of steel and stone. We, who were landless upon the land; we, who had barely managed to live in family groups; we, who needed the ritual and guidance of institutions to hold our atomized lives together in lines of purpose; we, who had known only relationships to people and not relationships to things; we, who had never belonged to any organization except the church and burial societies; we, who had had our personalities blasted with two hundred years of slavery and had been turned loose to shift for ourselves—we were such a folk as this when we moved into a world that was destined to test all we were, that threw us into the scales of competition to weight our mettle. And how were we to know that, the moment we landless millions of the land—we men who were struggling to be born—set our awkward feet upon the pavements of the city, life would begin to exact a heavy toll in death?

Ellen Wright and Michael Fabre, *The Richard Wright Reader*. New York: Harper & Row, 1978, p. 204.

spoken of yearning to get a seat on the New York Stock Exchange, his friends—in the boy's own interest—would have reported his odd ambition to the white boss. . . .

Planning the Move North

That winter my mother and brother came [to Memphis] and we set up housekeeping, buying furniture on the installment plan, being cheated and yet knowing no way to avoid it. I began to eat warm food and to my surprise found that regular meals enabled me to read faster. I may have lived through many illnesses and survived them, never suspecting that I was ill. My brother obtained a job and we began to save toward the trip north, plotting our time, setting tentative dates for departure. I told none of the white men on the job that I was planning to go north; I knew that the moment they felt I was thinking of the North they would change toward me. It would have made them feel that I did not like the life I was living, and because my life was completely conditioned by what they said or did, it would have been tantamount to challenging them.

I could calculate my chances for life in the South as a Negro fairly clearly now.

I could fight the southern whites by organizing with other Negroes, as my grandfather had done. But I knew that I could never win that way; there were many whites and there were but few blacks. They were strong and we were weak. Outright black rebellion could never win. If I fought openly I would die and I did not want to die. News of lynchings were frequent.

I could submit and live the life of a genial slave, but that was impossible. All of my life had shaped me to live by my own feelings and thoughts. I could make up to Bess and marry her and inherit the house. But that, too, would be the life of a slave; if I did that, I would crush to death something within me, and I would hate myself as much as I knew the whites already hated those who had submitted. Neither could I ever willingly present myself to be kicked, as Shorty had done. I would rather have died than do that.

I could drain off my restlessness by fighting with Shorty and Harrison. I had seen many Negroes solve the problem of being black by transferring their hatred of themselves to others with a black skin and fighting them. I would have to be cold to do that, and I was not cold and I could never be.

I could, of course, forget what I had read, thrust the whites out of my mind, forget them; and find release from anxiety and longing in sex and alcohol. But the memory of how my father had conducted himself made that course repugnant. If I did not want others to violate my life, how could I voluntarily violate it myself?

I had no hope whatever of being a professional man. Not only had I been so conditioned that I did not desire it, but the fulfillment of such an ambition was beyond my capabilities. Well-to-do Negroes lived in a world that was almost as alien to me as the world inhabited by whites.

What, then, was there? I held my life in my mind, in my consciousness each day, feeling at times that I would stumble and drop it, spill it forever. My reading had created a vast sense of distance between me and the world in which I lived and tried to make a living, and that sense of distance was increasing each day. My days and nights were one long, quiet, continuously contained dream of terror, tension, and anxiety. I wondered how long I could bear it.

Chapter 5

Martin Luther King's Forerunners

Chapter Preface

The black reformers who paved the road for the civil rights movement led by the Reverend Martin Luther King Jr. emerged during the Great Depression of the 1930s. In that economically troubled decade, African American labor leaders like A. Philip Randolph, organizer of the Brotherhood of Sleeping Car Porters (a union composed of black railroad porters), became a tireless advocate of equal wages and job opportunities for black Americans. His appeal to President Franklin D. Roosevelt led to a presidential order banning job discrimination in defense industries.

During the 1930s the National Association for the Advancement of Colored People (NAACP), through its Legal Defense Fund, began to challenge in court school segregation laws. Spearheaded by Thurgood Marshall, this effort opened to black students the doors of the University of Maryland School of Law in 1936 and the University of Missouri School of Law in 1938. After earning these victories, the NAACP would begin the battle to desegregate public elementary and high schools—an effort that culminated with the landmark Supreme Court decision in *Brown v. Board of Education of Topeka, Kansas,* which declared unconstitutional racial segregation in public schools.

World War II created opportunities for black reformers of the mid-twentieth century. The United States had waged that war, in part, to defeat the racist regime of Adolf Hitler in Nazi Germany. Thousands of African American soldiers, sailors, airmen, and nurses took part in that effort, but they returned home to a nation that was still strictly segregated along racial lines. Postwar African American civil rights leaders argued that it was hypocritical for Americans to condemn Hitler's racist policies and tolerate racism in their own country. In 1947 an army veteran, Jackie Robinson, broke major league baseball's color line when he took the field for the Brooklyn Dodgers. The following year President Harry Truman desegregated the U.S. armed forces.

The civil rights movement that King came to lead during the 1950s and 1960s had its roots in those desegregation efforts. The movement received its early momentum from the *Brown* case and from the Montgomery bus boycott, which was initiated by the actions of Rosa Parks and which presented King his first opportunity for leadership.

Integrating Major League Baseball

Jackie Robinson

Jackie Robinson had no intention of becoming a civil rights reformer; his goal was to play major league baseball. When he took the field for the Brooklyn Dodgers on April 15, 1947, however, he became a pioneer in the post–World War II effort to end racial segregation in the United States. On that date, Robinson became the first black major league baseball player of the twentieth century. Robinson blazed a trail for scores of black players who joined major league teams during the 1950s and changed the game of baseball. He also became a model for other reform-minded African Americans intent on integrating previously segregated workplaces, neighborhoods, schools, and public places. As this excerpt from his autobiography *I Never Had It Made* suggests, Robinson came under considerable pressure while achieving his goal. The Dodgers selected Robinson to integrate baseball because, in the view of Branch Rickey, the team's president, he had "the guts not to fight back" despite the racial taunts and curses hurled at him by those who wanted to keep baseball a white man's game.

E arly in the [1947] season, the Philadelphia Phillies came to Ebbets Field for a three-game series. I was still in my slump and events of the opening game certainly didn't help. Starting to the plate in the first inning, I could scarcely believe my ears. Almost as if it had been synchronized by some master conductor, hate poured forth from the Phillies dugout.

"Hey, nigger, why don't you go back to the cotton field where you belong?"

"They're waiting for you in the jungles, black boy!"

"Hey, snowflake, which one of those white boys' wives are you dating tonight?"

"We don't want you here, nigger."

"Go back to the bushes!"

Those insults and taunts were only samples of the torrent of abuse which poured out from the Phillies dugout that April day.

Dealing with Insults

I have to admit that this day of all the unpleasant days in my life, brought me nearer to cracking up than I ever had been. Perhaps I should have become inured to this kind of garbage, but I was in New York City and unprepared to face the kind of barbarism from a northern team that I had come to associate with the Deep South. The abuse coming out of the Phillies dugout was being directed by the team's manager, Ben Chapman, a Southerner. I felt tortured and I tried just to play ball and ignore the insults. But it was really getting to me. What did the Phillies want from me? What, indeed, did Mr. Rickey expect of me? I was, after all, a human being. What was I doing here turning the other cheek as though I weren't a man? In college days I had had a reputation as a black man who never tolerated affronts to his dignity. I had defied prejudice in the Army. How could I have thought that barriers would fall, that, indeed, my talent could triumph over bigotry?

For one wild and rage-crazed minute I thought, "To hell with Mr. Rickey's 'noble experiment.' It's clear it won't succeed. I have made every effort to work hard, to get myself into shape. My best is not enough for them." I thought what a glorious, cleansing thing it would be to let go. To hell with the image of the patient black freak I was supposed to create. I could throw down my bat, stride over to that Phillies dugout, grab one of those white sons of bitches and smash his teeth in with my despised black fist. Then I could walk away from it all. I'd never become a sports star. But my son could tell his son someday what his daddy could have been if he hadn't been too much of a man.

Then, I thought of Mr. Rickey—how his family and friends had begged him not to fight for me and my people. I thought of all his predictions, which had come true. Mr. Rickey had come to a crossroads and made a lonely decision. I was at a crossroads. I would make mine. I would stay.

The haters had almost won that round. They had succeeded in getting me so upset that I was an easy out. As the game progressed, the Phillies continued with the abuse.

After seven scoreless innings, we got the Phillies out in the eighth, and it was our turn at bat. I led off. The insults were still coming. I let the first pitch go by for a ball. I lined the next one into center field for a single. Gene Hermanski came up to hit and I took my lead.

The Phillies pitcher, a knuckle expert, let fly. I cut out for second. The throw was wide. It bounced past the shortstop. As I came into third, Hermanski singled me home. That was the game.

Apparently frustrated by our victory, the Phillies players kept the heat on me during the next two days. They even enlarged their name-calling to include the rest of the Brooklyn team.

"Hey, you carpetbaggers, how's your little reconstruction period getting along?"

Support from Teammates

That was a typical taunt. By the third day of our confrontation with these emissaries from the City of Brotherly Love, they had become so outrageous that Ed Stanky exploded. He started yelling at the Phillies.

"Listen, you yellow-bellied cowards," he cried out, "why don't you yell at somebody who can answer back?" It was then that I began to feel better. I remembered Mr. Rickey's prediction. If I won the respect of the team and got them solidly behind me, there would be no question about the success of the experiment.

Stanky wasn't the only Brooklyn player who was angry with the Phillies team. Some of my other teammates told the press about the way Chapman and his players had behaved. Sports columnists around the country criticized Chapman. Dan Parker, sports editor of the New York *Daily Mirror*, reported:

> Ben Chapman, who during his career with the Yankees was frequently involved in unpleasant incidents with fans who charged him with shouting anti-Semitic remarks at them from the ball field, seems to be up to his old trick of stirring up racial trouble. During the recent series between the Phils and the Dodgers, Chapman and three of his players poured a stream of abuse at Jackie Robinson. Jackie, with admirable restraint, ignored the guttersnipe language coming from the Phils dugout, thus stamping himself as the only gentleman among those involved in the incident.

Support from the Press

The black press did a real job of letting its readers know about the race baiting which had taken place. The publicity in the press built so much anti-Chapman public feeling that the Philadelphia club decided steps must be taken to counteract it. Chapman met with representatives of the black press to try to explain his behavior. The Phillies public relations people insisted, as Ben Chapman did, that he was not anti-Negro. Chapman himself used an interesting line of defense in speaking with black reporters. Didn't they want me to become a big-time big leaguer? Well, so did he and his players. When they played exhibitions with the Yanks, they razzed DiMaggio as "the Wop," Chapman explained. When they came up against the Cards, Whitey Kurowski was called "the Polack." Riding opposition players was the Phils' style of baseball. The Phils could give it out and they could take it. Was I a weakling who couldn't take it? Well, if I wasn't a weakling, then I shouldn't expect special treatment. After all, Chapman said, all is forgotten after a ball game ends.

The press, black and white, didn't buy that argument. They said so. Commissioner Happy Chandler wasn't having any either. His office warned the Phils to keep racial baiting out of the dugout bench jockeying.

Branch Rickey Stays the Course

A fascinating development of the nastiness with the Phils was the attitude of Mr. Rickey and the reaction of my Brooklyn teammates. Mr. Rickey knew, better than most people, that Chapman's racial prejudice was deeper than he admitted. Bob Carpenter, the Phils' president, had phoned Rickey before game time to try to persuade him not to include me in the lineup. If I played, Carpenter threatened, his team would refuse to play. Mr. Rickey's response was that this would be fine with him. The Dodgers would then take all three games by default. The Dodgers' president wasn't angry with Chapman or his players. As a matter of fact, in later years, Mr. Rickey commented, "Chapman did more than anybody to unite the Dodgers. When he poured out that string of unconscionable abuse, he solidified and unified thirty men, not one of whom was willing to sit by and see someone kick around a man who had his hands tied behind his back—Chapman made Jackie a real member of the Dodgers."

Privately, at the time, I thought Mr. Rickey was carrying his "gratitude" to Chapman a little too far when he asked me to appear in public with Chapman. The Phillies manager was genuinely in trouble as a result of all the publicity on the racial razzing. Mr. Rickey thought it would be gracious and generous if I posed for a picture shaking hands with Chapman. The idea was also promoted by the baseball commissioner. I was somewhat sold—but not altogether—on the concept that a display of such harmony would be "good for the game." I have to admit, though, that having my picture taken with this man was one of the most difficult things I had to make myself do.

An Anti-Robinson Plot

There were times, after I had bowed to humiliations like shaking hands with Chapman, when deep depression and speculation as to whether it was all worthwhile would seize me. Often, when I was in this kind of mood, something positive would happen to give me new strength. Sometimes the positive development would come in response to a negative one. This was exactly what happened when a clever sports editor exposed a plot that was brewing among the St. Louis Cardinals. The plan was set to be executed on May 9, 1947, when Brooklyn was to visit St. Louis for the first game of the season between the two clubs. The Cards were planning to pull a last-minute protest strike against my playing in the game. If successful, the plan could have had a chain reac-

A Labor Leader Articulates African Americans' Fight for Equal Rights

Asa Philip Randolph, founder of the Brotherhood of Sleeping Car Porters, connected anti-Negro sentiment in the South with the oppression of Jews in Nazi Europe in a 1942 article in Survey Graphic.

A community is democratic only when the humblest and weakest person can enjoy the highest civil, economic, and social rights that the biggest and most powerful possess. To trample on these rights of both Negroes and poor whites is such a commonplace in the South that it takes readily to antisocial, antilabor, anti-Semitic, and anti-Catholic propaganda. It was because of laxness in enforcing the Weimer Constitution in republican Germany that Nazism made headway. Oppression of the Negroes in the United States, like the suppression of the Jews in Germany, may open the way for a fascist dictatorship.

By fighting for their rights now, American Negroes are helping to make America a moral and spiritual arsenal of democracy. Their fight against the poll tax, against lynch law, segregation, and Jim Crow, their fight for economic, political, and social equality, thus becomes part of the global war for freedom.

Sanford Wexler, *The Civil Rights Movement: An Eyewitness History.* New York: Facts On File, 1993, p. 26.

tion throughout the baseball world—with other players agreeing to unite in a strong bid to keep baseball white. Stanley Woodward, sports editor of the New York *Herald Tribune,* had learned of the plot and printed an exclusive scoop exposing it. [National League president] Ford Frick reacted immediately and notified the Cardinal players in no uncertain terms that they would not be permitted to get away with a strike.

"If you do this you will be suspended from the league," Frick warned. "You will find that the friends you think you have in the press box will not support you, that you will be outcasts. I do not care if half the league strikes. Those who do it will encounter quick retribution. They will be suspended and I don't care if it wrecks the National League for five years. This is the United States of America, and one citizen has as much right to play as another.

"The National League," Frick continued, "will go down the line with Robinson whatever the consequence. You will find if you go through with your intention that you have been guilty of complete madness."

The hot light of publicity about the plot and the forthright hard line that Frick laid down to the plotters helped to avert what could have been a disaster for integration of baseball. Many writers and baseball personalities credited Woodward with significant service to baseball and to sportsmanship.

Hate Mail and Threats

While some positive things were happening, there were others that were negative. Hate mail arrived daily, but it didn't bother me nearly as much as the threat mail. The threat mail included orders to me to get out of the game or be killed, threats to assault Rachel, to kidnap Jackie, Jr. Although none of the threats materialized, I was quite alarmed. Mr. Rickey, early in May, decided to turn some of the letters over to the police.

That same spring the Benjamin Franklin Hotel in Philadelphia, where my teammates were quartered, refused to accommodate me. The Phillies heckled me a second time, mixing up race baiting with childish remarks and gestures that coincided with the threats that had been made. Some of those grown men sat in the dugout and pointed bats at me and made machine-gunlike noises. It was an incredibly childish display of bad will.

Support from a Special Teammate

I was helped over these crises by the courage and decency of a teammate who could easily have been my enemy rather than my friend. Pee Wee Reese, the successful Dodger shortstop, was one of the most highly respected players in the major leagues. When I first joined the club, I was aware that there might well be a real reluctance on Reese's part to accept me as a teammate. He was from Ekron, Kentucky. Furthermore, it had been rumored that I might take over Reese's position on the team. Mischief-makers seeking to create trouble between us had tried to agitate Reese into regarding me as a threat—a black one at that. But Reese, from the time I joined Brooklyn, had demonstrated a totally fair attitude.

Reese told a sportswriter, some months after I became a Dodger, "When I first met Robinson in spring training, I figured, well, let me give this guy a chance. It may be he's just as good as I am. Frankly, I don't think I'd stand up under the kind of thing he's been subjected to as well as he has."

Reese's tolerant attitude of witholding judgment to see if I would make it was translated into positive support soon after we became teammates. In Boston during a period when the heckling pressure seemed unbearable, some of the Boston players began to heckle Reese. They were riding him about being a Southerner and playing ball with a black man. Pee Wee didn't answer them. Without a glance in their direction, he left his position and walked over to me. He put his hand on my shoulder and began talking to me. His words weren't important. I don't even remember what he said. It was the gesture of comradeship and support that counted. As he stood talking with me with a friendly arm around my shoulder, he was saying loud and clear, "Yell. Heckle. Do anything you want. We came here to play baseball."

The jeering stopped, and a close and lasting friendship began between Reese and me. We were able, not only to help each other and our team in private as well as public situations, but to talk about racial prejudices and misunderstanding.

A Loner

At the same time Mr. Rickey told me that when my teammates began to rally to my cause, we could consider the battle half won; he had also said that one of my roughest burdens would be the experience of being lonely in the midst of a group—my teammates. They would be my teammates on the field. But back in the locker rooms, I would know the strain and pressure of being a stranger in a crowd of guys who were friendly among themselves but uncertain about how to treat me. Some of them would resent me but would cover the resentment with aloofness or just a minimum amount of courtesy. Others genuinely wouldn't know how to be friendly with me. Some would even feel I preferred to be off in a corner and left out. After the games were over, my teammates had normal social lives with their wives, their girls, and each other. When I traveled, during those early days, unless Wendell Smith or some other black sportswriter happened to be going along, I sat by myself while the other guys chatted and laughed and played cards. I remember vividly a rare occasion when I was invited to join a poker game. One of the participants was a Georgia guy, Hugh Casey, the relief pitcher. Casey's luck wasn't too good during the game, and at one point he addressed a remark directly to me that caused a horrified silence.

"You know what I used to do down in Georgia when I ran into bad luck?" he said. "I used to go out and find me the biggest, blackest nigger woman I could find and rub her teats to change my luck."

I don't believe there was a man in that game, including me, who thought that I could take that. I had to force back my anger. I had the memory of Mr. Rickey's words about looking for a man "with guts enough not to fight back." Finally, I made myself turn to the dealer and told him to deal the cards.

The Effort to Desegregate America's Public Schools

Thurgood Marshall

Some historians would argue that the civil rights movement that Reverend Martin Luther King Jr. spearheaded during the 1950s and 1960s began with the Supreme Court's decision in the landmark 1954 case of *Brown v. Board of Education of Topeka, Kansas.* That decision outlawed segregation in public schools and established a precedent for lower courts to invalidate laws that segregated other public places such as beaches, parks, golf courses, and bus terminals. Thurgood Marshall was the leading attorney for the National Association for the Advancement of Colored People (NAACP) in the *Brown* case. A product of Baltimore's segregated public schools, Marshall earned degrees from Lincoln University and Howard University School of Law, traditional black institutions. Shortly after being admitted to the bar, Marshall went to work for the NAACP's Legal Defense Fund and began to test segregation laws in the courts. In this excerpt from an article that originally appeared in *Journal of Negro Education* in 1952, Marshall describes the efforts that his organization was making to desegregate public elementary and high schools. Thirteen years after the *Brown* decision, Marshall became the first African American to occupy a seat on the U.S. Supreme Court.

While the right of Negroes to attend state graduate and professional schools has now been established, most Negroes who have received their early education in segregated schools are handicapped because their early training was inadequate and inferior. It became increasingly apparent that the supreme test would have to be made—an attack on segregation at the elementary and high school levels. Acceptance of segregation under the "separate but equal" doctrine had become so ingrained that overwhelming proof was sorely needed to demonstrate that equal educational opportunities for Negroes could not be provided in a segregated system.

The Effect of Segregated Schools

It is relatively easy to show that a Negro graduate student offered training in a separate school, thrown up overnight, could not get an education equal to that available at the state universities. Public elementary and high schools, however, present a more difficult basis for comparison. They are normally not specialized institutions with national or even statewide reputations. Public school teachers at these levels are not likely to gain eminence in the profession comparable to that of teachers in colleges and universities. For years, however, exposure of the evils of segregation and discrimination has come from social scientists, and their help was elicited for this phase of the campaign. Social scientists are almost in universal agreement that segregated education produces inequality. Studies have been made of the personality problems caused by discrimination and segregation and most social scientists have reached the conclusion that artificial and arbitrary barriers, such as race and color bars, are likely to have an adverse effect on the personality development of the individual. The energy and strength which the individual might otherwise use in the development of his mental resources is dissipated in adjustment to the problems of segregation.

Unfortunately, the effects of segregation in education have not been isolated for study by social scientists. They have dealt with the whole problem of segregation, discrimination and prejudice, and although no social scientist can say that segregated schools alone give the Negro feelings of insecurity, self-hate, undermine his ego, make him feel inferior and warp his outlook on life, yet for the child the school provides the most important contact with organized society. What he learns, feels, and how he is affected there is apt to determine the type of adult he will become. Social scientists have found that children at a very early age are affected by and react to discrimination and prejudices. Thus they have agreed that it is sound to conclude that segregated schools, perhaps more than any other single factor, are of major concern to the individual of public school age and contributes greatly to the unwholesomeness and unhappy development of the personality of Negroes which the color caste system in the United States has produced.

The elimination of segregation in public schools may not remove all of the causes of insecurity, self-hate, etc., among Negroes, but since this is a state-sponsored program, certainly the state, consistent with the requirements of the Fourteenth Amendment, should not be a party to a system which does help produce these results. This is the thesis which is now being used to demonstrate the unconstitutionality of segregation at the public elementary and high school levels.

Test Cases

Preliminary test cases in Virginia and Texas demonstrated the ineffectiveness of the failure to push for a clear-cut determination of the validity of the segregation statutes. I believe that an appraisal of these cases will show that their success was limited by the same difficulties as were encountered in the earlier university cases. After considerable and costly litigation and appeals, these cases ended in court orders limited to the equalization of physical facilities. These facilities in each instance were not equalized so that it was necessary to file motions for further relief to reopen the cases for a new determination of whether or not the Fourteenth Amendment was being complied with. It is significant that in these latter proceedings it was found necessary to make a frontal attack on the validity of segregated statutes.

The *Clarendon County School* case was the first test case to make a direct attack against segregation on the elementary and high school level. That case, which was tried in Charleston, South Carolina in May of last year, was based upon the theory that the *Sweatt* and *McLaurin* decisions have pointed the way toward consideration of the validity of segregation on all levels of education. In order to extend this principle it was necessary to produce equally competent testimony to show the unreasonableness of segregation and the impossibility of equality of Jim Crow education on the lower levels.

Therefore, in the *Clarendon County* case competent expert testimony was produced to show that segregation on the elementary and high school levels was just as unequal as segregated education on the graduate and professional school level when measured by the criteria set forth in the *Sweatt* and *McLaurin* decisions. In other words, competent expert testimony was produced to show in detail the injury to the Negro pupil attending the segregated schools in Clarendon County and to show that this injury was a permanent and continuing one which prevented the Negro child from obtaining an education equal to that obtained by other students. Of course, testimony was also produced to show that there was no reasonable basis for racial segregation in public education. Two of the three judges deciding this case held that despite this testimony the separate-but-equal doctrine was still a valid doctrine supported by decisions of the Supreme Court and that although the schools were not equal in physical facilities, the Negroes were entitled to equal facilities and they should be given equal physical facilities. The majority of the court therefore refused to enjoin enforcement of the segregation statutes of South Carolina but ordered that the physical facilities be equalized and ordered the school board to report within six months on this equalization of physical facilities. Judge J. Waties Waring, however, in a most vigorous dissenting opinion held that the segregation laws were unconstitutional and stated that segregation was per se unconstitutional. A direct appeal from the majority judgment was made to the United States Supreme Court where, on January 26, 1952, the United States Supreme Court issued an order vacating the judgment of the lower court and remanding the case to that court for a consideration of the report made by the school officials and any other additional facts in order that the district court "be afforded the opportunity to take whatever action it may deem appropriate in light of that report."

A hearing was promptly held in the district court with Judge Dobie of Virginia replacing Judge Waring, who had previously retired from the Bench. After argument, the new three-judge court issued a unanimous decree again refusing to declare the statutes unconstitutional but again ordering the school board to furnish equal facilities. An appeal is now being prepared to the Supreme Court from this latest decision.

The second case in this line of cases is the *Topeka, Kansas* case which was tried in June of last year. Again similar testimony from other expert witnesses in larger number was produced and in this case the three judges unanimously found as a fact that:

> Segregation of white and colored children in public schools has a detrimental effect upon the colored children. The impact is greater when it has the sanction of the law; for the policy of separating the races is usually interpreted as denoting inferiority of the Negro group. A sense of inferiority affects the motivation of a child to learn. Segregation with the sanction of law, therefore, has a tendency to retard the education and mental development of Negro children and to deprive them of some of the benefits they would receive in a racial integrated school system.

The same court, however, felt obliged not to follow this finding but to follow the antiquated decisions of the Supreme Court which seem to uphold the validity of segregation in elementary education. That case is now pending before the United States Supreme Court.

The third case was the *Wilmington, Delaware* case which was tried on October 22, 1951 and which was decided week before last in an exhaustive twenty-six page opinion by Chancellor Collins J. Seitz ordering the admission of the Negroes in the previously all white schools.

The fourth case was the *Prince Edward, Virginia* case tried before a three-judge court in Richmond, Virginia last month. In this case which was tried for a full week more expert testimony was produced than in any other of the cases. For the first time the other side produced expert testimony which while opposing the immediate removal of segregation nevertheless admitted the inequality inherent in a segregated school system in addition to the regular inequalities in physical equipment. This court in unanimous opinion refused to enjoin the segregation statutes but ordered the equalization of physical facilities. This case is also being prepared for appeal to the United States Supreme Court. . . .

Reaction to the Test Cases

I will, of course, not speculate as to either the outcome of the individual cases or the general decision of the Supreme Court on this point. Getting back to an appraisal of the recent cases in the line of the objective sought, we can appraise these cases in the light of their immediate effect. In South Carolina, Governor Byrnes in an effort to circumvent these cases, last year succeeded in getting through the legislature approval for a seventy-five million dollar school fund based upon a sales tax. This seventy-five million dollars will be used in both Negro and white schools. It is admitted that this fund is for the purpose of equalizing physical facilities, a large proportion of the fund will no doubt go to white schools. At any rate, if nothing more is done in the legal field, the schools of South Carolina both Negro and white will be seventy-five million dollars better off. On the other hand, Governor Byrnes followed by Governor Talmadge of Georgia had put through a plan whereby they hope to turn over the public schools to private institutions such as churches in the event that the Supreme Court declares the segregation statutes invalid. Many of us are convinced that this move to turn over the public schools to private institutions will be declared invalid by the Supreme Court. There are even more people who are convinced that the white citizens in these states are not insane enough on the segregation issue to be willing to turn over millions of dollars of their tax money invested in schools to private institutions where they will have little, if any, control over the education of their children.

Many of the people who believe that segregation is invalid and should be declared unconstitutional are moved by this threat of a few Southern governors. It seems to me that the best answer to this threat is that the same threat was made by the attorneys-general of the Southern states while the *Sweatt* and *McLaurin* cases were pending in the Supreme Court. The specific threat was that if segregation was destroyed on the graduate and professional level "the states are left with no alternative but to close their schools to prevent violence." The record shows that no state universities were closed and nothing happened except that Negroes were admitted just as if they had been attending the schools for years back. In the face of these facts, the argument is now made that elementary and high school education is different and that the South will not stand for it. There is an answer

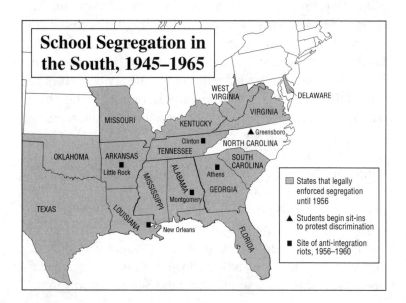

School Segregation in the South, 1945–1965

to this argument also. Many junior colleges in Texas have recently opened their doors to Negroes and nothing happened. This brings us to another phase of the objective of this litigation and that is the education of the general public to the evils of segregation, its harmful effects and the reasons why this segregation should be abolished.

The pendency of the *Sipuel, Sweatt,* and *McLaurin* cases over a period of some five years brought about wide newspaper coverage and discussion in daily press, the weekly magazine, the professional magazines and college newspapers. This education of the general public played a large part in making it possible for the Negro students to be admitted without incident, to have no trouble while in school, and to encourage other public and private colleges and universities to open their doors to qualified Negroes.

The pending cases have likewise received wide and broad coverage in the same channels. In addition, articles are now appearing in scientific journals on the validity of the scientific testimony in this field. It is doubtful that this issue will be resolved over night but the pendency of these cases will continue to educate the general public along the lines suggested above.

It has been most encouraging to find that whereas the earlier cases on the university level failed to attract the attention and support of most of the Negro communities, the present litigation has had 100 per cent cooperation in each area where these cases have been pending. For example, the courage of the Negroes in Clarendon County, South Carolina, and the support of the Negroes in other areas in South Carolina; the courage of the Negroes in Farmville, Virginia and the support from the other areas in Virginia will stand as a landmark in the struggle for full citizenship. Any appraisal of the actual cases in these fields must include an appraisal of the community support commanded by the cases.

A Step-By-Step Approach to Desegregation

Neither the *Sipuel* nor the *McLaurin* decisions struck down the separate-but-equal doctrine. There are many who hoped that this would happen. However, all legal minds will agree that the Supreme Court is not obliged to make far sweeping decisions but rather tends to limit its decision to the matter before it in the pending cases. So it is apparent that the whole segregation problem cannot be solved in one law suit. It would, of course, be easier and cheaper to do it that way. If we view the problem from a realistic standpoint, it means that the best possible course is a step-by-step approach on each level of education to be followed by a step-by-step approach at each other area of segregation.

In addition, it is necessary to implement the precedents on each level and this will require additional law suits on each level. The present cases on the elementary and high school level show the varied approach to this problem, varied as to area, and varied as to testimony.

The university cases not only opened the state universities in twelve Southern states but many private institutions in states like Kentucky and Maryland have opened their doors to qualified Negroes. There are other private colleges willing to open their doors to Negroes but are prevented from doing so by state statutes. It is expected that in the near future there will be cases filed to enjoin the enforcement of these statutes as applied to the private colleges anxious to admit qualified Negroes. There has also been some discussion as to the eventual possibility in the future of requiring a private college to admit Negro students despite its ban upon the admission of Negro students. I imagine that this suggestion when and if made will split the legal profession in half.

In states like Alabama, Florida, South Carolina and Mississippi, the time when the universities in these states will be opened to Negroes depend solely upon when qualified Negroes apply to those universities, and are refused admission and bring suit against these universities. As soon as that is done they will be opened up. Such a case is now ready for filing in Georgia and it is expected that additional cases will be filed in Florida in order to open up the University of Florida.

Our Primary Objective

The primary objective of this recent litigation has been to obtain full and complete integration of all students on all levels of public education without regard to race or color. The stumbling block in the path toward this objective is the separate-but-equal doctrine. In the beginning the Courts prevented litigants from either attacking the doctrine head on or circumventing the doctrine. In the next phase of this program the courts eventually permitted the tangential approach by ordering equality of physical facilities while upholding segregation.

Finally in the *Sweatt* and *McLaurin* decisions the tangential approach was discarded and segregation on the graduate and professional school levels was removed. Even there the Supreme Court refused to strike down the separate-but-equal doctrine as such. The elementary and high school cases are the next steps in this campaign toward the objective and complete integration of all students.

The earlier legal approach to this problem failed to bring about either integration or equality of physical facilities. The direct attack on segregation even if successful in its all-out attack on segregation nevertheless produces immediate serious efforts toward physical equality.

In evaluating these recent cases we must always bear in mind that we are dealing with a brand new field of law both as to substantive law and procedural law. Although the separate-but-equal doctrine still stands in the road blocking full equality or opportunity, recent cases have been closing the doors of escape from a clear-cut determination of the validity or invalidity of this doctrine. While evaluating the recent decisions we must constantly look to the future.

Desegregating Montgomery's Buses

Rosa Parks

> The Montgomery Bus Boycott propelled Reverend Martin Luther King Jr. to a leadership position in the civil rights movement. The boycott began when Rosa Parks, a forty-three-year-old seamstress and the secretary for the NAACP chapter in Montgomery, Alabama, refused to surrender her bus seat to a white passenger, as required by law. Parks was arrested and fined $14 for her offense. Her arrest, however, energized Montgomery's black residents, who had long opposed the law that made them relinquish their seats to white passengers. A successful bus boycott, led by King, that captivated the entire nation ensued—the first noteworthy and successful civil rights protest in the American South. During the next decade, King led the battle to desegregate restaurants, hotels, movie theaters, and other public places previously segregated by law. For her effort, Parks has become known as the mother or grandmother of the civil rights movement. This excerpt from Parks's book *Quiet Strength* details her actions on December 1, 1955.

After the 1954 Supreme Court ruling on *Brown v. Board of Education*, which designated separate-but-equal schools for children unlawful, a few people felt optimistic that things would get better. The laws were changed, but the heart of America remained unchanged.

One day I noticed a little child whose mother was taking

him to one of the integrated schools. From the nervous look on his face I could tell he did not want to go to that white school, and his mother, she did not know what was going to happen. It was not easy for a small child to walk into a place of merely token integration, where a multitude of white persons had always been taught there should be racial segregation.

Despite the banning of separate schools for the races, most people did not react too favorably. They were more indifferent than interested. It was not easy, you see, because the pattern had existed so long. There were still separate elevators and fountains for white and colored people. I used them as little as possible.

The more I became involved with the NAACP, the more I learned of discrimination and acts of violence against blacks, such as lynchings, rapes, and unsolved murders. And the more I learned about these incidents, the more I felt I could no longer passively sit by and accept the Jim Crow laws. A better day had to come.

Riding Segregated Buses

The custom for getting on the bus for black persons in Montgomery in 1955 was to pay at the front door, get off the bus, and then re-enter through the back door to find a seat. On the buses, if white persons got on, the colored would move back if the white section was filled. Black people could not sit in the same row with white people. They could not even sit across the aisle from each other. Some customs were humiliating, and this one was intolerable since we were the majority of the ridership.

On Thursday evening, December 1, I was riding the bus home from work. A white man got on, and the driver looked our way and said, "Let me have those seats." It did not seem proper, particularly for a woman to give her seat to a man. All the passengers paid ten cents, just as he did. When more whites boarded the bus, the driver, J.P. Blake, ordered the blacks in the fifth row, the first row of the colored section (the row I was sitting in), to move to the rear. Bus drivers then had police powers, under both municipal and state laws, to enforce racial segregation. However, we were sitting in the section designated for colored.

At first none of us moved.

"Y'all better make it light on yourselves and let me have those seats," Blake said.

Then three of the blacks in my row got up, but I stayed in my seat and slid closer to the window. I do not remember being frightened. But I sure did not believe I would "make it light" on myself by standing up. Our mistreatment was just not right, and I was tired of it. The more we gave in, the worse they treated us. I kept thinking about my mother and my grandparents, and how strong they were. I knew there was a possibility of being mistreated, but an opportunity was being given to me to do what I had asked of others.

Taking the First Step

I knew someone had to take the first step. So I made up my mind not to move. Blake asked me if I was going to stand up.

"No. I am not," I answered.

Blake said that he would have to call the police. I said, "Go ahead." In less than five minutes, two policemen came, and the driver pointed me out. He said that he wanted the seat and that I would not stand up.

"Why do you push us around?" I said to one of the policemen.

"I don't know," he answered, "but the law is the law and you're under arrest."

I did not get on the bus to get arrested; I got on the bus to go home. Getting arrested was one of the worst days in my life. It was not a happy experience. Since I have always been a strong believer in God, I knew that He was with me, and only He could get me through the next step.

I had no idea that history was being made. I was just tired of giving in. Somehow, I felt that what I did was right by standing up to that bus driver. I did not think about the consequences. I knew that I could have been lynched, manhandled, or beaten when the police came. I chose not to move.

When I made that decision, I knew that I had the strength of my ancestors with me.

There were other people on the bus whom I knew. But when I was arrested, not one of them came to my defense. I felt very much alone. One man who knew me did not even go by my house to tell my husband I had been arrested. Everyone just went on their way.

In jail I felt even more alone. For a moment, as I sat in that little room with bars, before I was moved to a cell with two other women, I felt that I had been deserted. But I did not cry. I said a silent prayer and waited.

Later that evening, to my great relief, I was released. It is strange: after the arrest, I never did reach the breaking point of shedding tears. The next day, I returned to work. It was pouring down rain, so I called a cab. The young man at work was so surprised to see me. He thought I would be too nervous and shaken to go back to work.

Three days later I was found guilty and ordered to pay a ten-dollar fine plus four dollars in court costs. The case was later appealed with the help of one of my attorneys, Fred Gray, and I did not have to pay anything.

It is funny to me how people came to believe that the reason that I did not move from my seat was that my feet were tired. I did not hear this until I moved to Detroit in 1957. My feet were not tired, but *I* was tired—tired of unfair treatment. I also heard later that Mother Pollard, one of the marchers in Montgomery, said that my feet were tired but my soul was rested. She was right about my soul.

The Bus Boycott

On Monday, December 5, the day I went to court, the Montgomery Improvement Association (MIA) was formed to start the bus boycott. It is sad, in a way, to think about what we had to go through to get to that point. We, as a people, all felt discouraged with our situation, but we had not been united enough to conquer it. Now, the fearfulness and bitterness was turning into power.

So the people started organizing, protesting, and walking.

Many thousands were willing to sacrifice the comfort and convenience of riding the bus. This was the modern mass movement we needed. I suppose they were showing sympathy for a person who had been mistreated. It was not just my arrest that year. Many African-Americans, including Emmet Till, had been killed or beaten for racist reasons. I was the third woman in Montgomery to be arrested on a bus. We reached the point where we simply had to take action.

Nearly a year later the segregated-bus ordinance was declared unconstitutional by the U.S. Supreme Court. One day after the boycott ended, I rode a nonsegregated bus for the first time.

A month after the boycott began, I lost my twenty-five-dollar-a-week job when the now-defunct Montgomery Fair department store closed its tailor shop. I was given no indication from the store that my boycott activities were the reason I lost my job. People always wanted to say it was because of my involvement in the boycott. I cannot say this is true. I do not like to form in my mind something I do not have any proof of.

A Movement of Many

Four decades later I am still uncomfortable with the credit given to me for starting the bus boycott. Many people do not know the whole truth; I would like them to know I was not the only person involved. I was just one of many who fought for freedom. And many others around me began to *want* to fight for their rights as well.

At that time, the Reverend Martin Luther King Jr. was emerging on the scene. He once said, "If you will protest courageously and yet with dignity and Christian love, when the history books are written in future generations, the historians will have to pause and say: there lived a great people—a black people—who injected new meaning and dignity into the veins of civilization." It was these words that guided many of us as we faced the trials and tribulations of fighting for our rights.

Chronology

1619
Slavery is introduced to North America at the British colony in Jamestown, Virginia.

1783
Great Britain grants independence to its thirteen American colonies, but slavery remains in place; by 1804, however, slavery is outlawed in all states north of the Mason-Dixon Line.

1789
Olaudah Equiano, a former slave and an abolitionist active in the movement to outlaw international slave trading, publishes *The Interesting Narrative of the Life of Olaudah Equiano,* the first slave narrative written by a former slave.

1808
The U.S. Congress outlaws the importation of slaves; slave trading remains legal within the United States.

1829
David Walker, a black abolitionist freeman, publishes *David Walker's Appeal, in Four Articles,* an abolitionist tract.

1831
William Lloyd Garrison, a white abolitionist from Boston, begins publication of *The Liberator,* an antislavery newspaper; Nat Turner begins a slave rebellion in Southampton County, Virginia; the rebellion is broken after a single day of violence; Turner is eventually captured, tried, and executed; Thomas R. Gray, an attorney who interviewed Turner, publishes *The Confessions of Nat Turner.*

1833
Garrison and his followers establish the American Anti-Slavery Society.

1841
Frederick Douglass, a fugitive slave, begins delivering speeches for the American Anti-Slavery Society.

1845
Douglass publishes *Narrative of the Life of Frederick Douglass, an American Slave.*

1850
Olive Gilbert publishes *Narrative of Sojourner Truth,* the life story of a former slave who became a nationally known abolitionist orator.

1861
The Civil War begins; President Abraham Lincoln insists that the war is being fought to restore the Union, not to abolish slavery; Douglass and other abolitionists urge Lincoln to make slavery one of the casualties of the war.

1863
President Lincoln issues the Emancipation Proclamation, which frees all slaves in the states in rebellion against the Union.

1865
The Civil War ends; the Thirteenth Amendment of the U.S. Constitution is adopted, prohibiting slavery in the United States and its territories.

1868
The Fourteenth Amendment is adopted, making all individuals born in the United States citizens of the nation and their states of residence and guaranteeing all citizens "equal protection of the laws."

1870

The Fifteenth Amendment is adopted, prohibiting Congress and individual states from denying citizens the right to vote because of race, color, or previous condition of servitude.

1881

Booker T. Washington, a former slave, is appointed president of the Tuskegee Institute in Alabama, a school that provides vocational training for black students.

1895

Washington delivers his Atlanta Exposition address.

1896

The U.S. Supreme Court decides the case of *Plessy v. Ferguson,* which establishes the doctrine of "separate but equal"; laws that segregate the races in public places remain in force.

1901

Washington publishes *Up from Slavery.*

1903

Harvard-educated W.E.B. DuBois publishes *The Souls of Black Folk.*

1909

DuBois and his followers establish the National Association for the Advancement of Colored People (NAACP), the most influential civil rights organization of the twentieth century.

1914

Marcus Garvey forms the Universal Negro Improvement Association.

1925

Asa Philip Randolph, a black train porter, establishes the Brotherhood of Sleeping Car Porters, a union certified by the American Federation of Labor.

1929
The Great Depression begins, causing strife and poverty in black urban and rural communities.

1936
Thurgood Marshall, an NAACP attorney, successfully sues the University of Maryland School of Law, forcing the institution to admit qualified black students.

1938
As a result of an NAACP lawsuit brought by Marshall, the U.S. Supreme Court desegregates the University of Missouri School of Law.

1941
The United States enters World War II; thousands of black Americans participate in the war effort.

1945
World War II ends; Richard Wright publishes his autobiography, *Black Boy,* his story of growing up in the Jim Crow South.

1947
Jackie Robinson integrates major league baseball.

1948
President Harry Truman integrates the U.S. armed forces.

1954
The Supreme Court outlaws racial segregation in public schools in the case of *Brown v. Board of Education of Topeka, Kansas;* the plaintiffs' case was advanced by the NAACP.

1955
Rosa Parks, a Montgomery, Alabama, seamstress, is arrested for refusing to surrender her bus seat to a white passenger, as prescribed by law; the Montgomery bus boycott begins, with the Reverend Martin Luther King Jr. as its leader.

For Further Research

General Histories of the Civil Rights Movement

Robert H. Brisbane, *The Black Vanguard: Origins of the Negro Social Revolution, 1900–1960.* Valley Forge, PA: Judson, 1970.

Merton L. Dillon, *The Abolitionists: The Growth of a Dissenting Minority.* Dekalb: Northern Illinois University Press, 1974.

John Egerton, *Speak Now Against the Day: The Generation Before the Civil Rights Movement in the South.* New York: Alfred A. Knopf, 1995.

Adam Fairclough, *Better Day Coming: Blacks and Equality, 1890–2000.* New York: Viking, 2001.

Minnie Finch, *The NAACP: Its Fight for Justice.* Metuchen, NJ: Scarecrow, 1981.

Eric Foner, *Nothing but Freedom: Emancipation and Its Legacy.* Baton Rouge: Louisiana State University Press, 1983.

———, *Reconstruction: America's Unfinished Revolution, 1863–1877.* New York: Harper and Row, 1988.

———, *Slavery, the Civil War, and Reconstruction.* Washington, DC: American Historical Association, 1990.

John Hope Franklin, *From Slavery to Freedom: A History of Negro Americans.* New York: Alfred A. Knopf, 1968.

———, *Reconstruction After the Civil War.* Chicago: University of Chicago Press, 1961.

Langston Hughes, *Fight for Freedom: The Story of the NAACP.* New York: W.W. Norton, 1962.

Richard Kluger, *Simple Justice: The History of "Brown v. Board of Education" and Black America's Struggle for Equality.* New York: Alfred A. Knopf, 1976.

Leon Litwack, *Been in the Storm So Long: The Aftermath of Slavery.* New York: Vintage Books, 1980.

James M. McPherson, *The Abolitionist Legacy: From Reconstruction to the NAACP.* Princeton, NJ: Princeton University Press, 1975.

———, *The Struggle for Equality: Abolitionists and the Negro in the Civil War and Reconstruction.* Princeton, NJ: Princeton University Press, 1964.

Milton Meltzer, *In Their Own Words: A History of the American Negro, 1865–1916.* New York: Crowell, 1965.

Jerrold M. Packard, *American Nightmare: The History of Jim Crow.* New York: St. Martin's, 2002.

Benjamin Quarles, *The Black Abolitionists.* New York: Oxford University Press, 1969.

Sanford Wexler, *The Civil Rights Movement: An Eyewitness History.* New York: Facts On File, 1993.

C. Vann Woodward, *The Strange Career of Jim Crow.* 3rd ed. rev. New York: Oxford University Press, 1974.

Richard Wright, "The Ethics of Living Jim Crow," in *Uncle Tom's Children.* New York: Harper and Row, 1989.

Texts on Individual Black Reformers

William Andrews, ed., *New Essays on W.E.B. DuBois.* Cambridge, England: Cambridge University Press, 1985.

David W. Blight, *Frederick Douglass's Civil War: Keeping Faith in Jubilee.* Baton Rouge: Louisiana State University Press, 1989.

Melba Joyce Boyd, *Discarded Legacy: Politics and Poetics in the Life of Frances E.W. Harper.* Detroit, MI: Wayne State University Press, 1994.

Edmund David Cronon, *Black Moses: The Story of Marcus Garvey and the Universal Negro Improvement Association.* Madison: University of Wisconsin Press, 1962.

Michael Fabre, *The World of Richard Wright.* Jackson: University Press of Mississippi, 1985.

Roger Goldman and David Gallen, *Thurgood Marshall: Justice for All.* New York: Carroll & Graf, 1992.

Louis R. Harlan, *Booker T. Washington: The Making of a Black Leader, 1856–1901.* New York: Oxford University Press, 1972.

———, *Booker T. Washington: The Wizard of Tuskegee, 1901–1915.* New York: Oxford University Press, 1983.

Peter P. Hinks, *To Awaken My Afflicted Brethren: David Walker and the Problem of Antebellum Slave Resistance.* University Park: Pennsylvania State University Press, 1996.

Nathan Irwin Huggins, *Slave and Citizen: The Life of Frederick Douglass.* Boston: Little, Brown, 1980.

David Levering Lewis, *W.E.B. DuBois: Biography of a Race, 1868–1919.* New York: Holt, 1993.

Paula F. Pfeffer, *A. Philip Randolph: Pioneer of the Civil Rights Movement.* Baton Rouge: Louisiana State University Press, 1990.

Arnold Rampersad, *The Art and Imagination of W.E.B. DuBois.* Cambridge, MA: Harvard University Press, 1976.

Jo Ann Robinson, *The Montgomery Bus Boycott and the Women Who Started It.* Ed. David J. Garrow. Knoxville: University of Tennessee Press, 1987.

Dorothy Sterling, *Black Foremothers: Three Lives.* New York: Feminist, 1988.

Erlene Stetson, *Glorying in Tribulation: The Lifework of Sojourner Truth.* East Lansing: Michigan State University Press, 1994.

Jules Tygiel, *Baseball's Great Experiment: Jackie Robinson and His Legacy.* New York: Oxford University Press, 1983.

James Walvin, *An African's Life: The Life and Times of Olaudah Equiano, 1745–1797.* Washington, DC: Cassell, 1998.

Collections of Documents

Albert P. Blaustein and Robert L. Zangrando, eds., *Civil Rights and the American Negro: A Documentary History.* New York: Trident, 1968.

Joanne Grant, ed., *Black Protest: History, Documents, and Analyses, 1619 to the Present.* New York: Fawcett, 1968.

Emma Lou Thornbrough, ed., *Black Reconstructionists.* Englewood Cliffs, NJ: Prentice-Hall, 1972.

Cary D. Wintz, ed., *African American Political Thought: Washington, DuBois, Garvey, and Randolph.* Armonk, NY: M.E. Sharpe, 1996.

Index